# VISIBLE UNKNOWN

AARON LI

VISIBLE UNKNOWN

Aaron Li

ISBN (Print Edition): 978-1-66783-526-6

ISBN (eBook Edition): 978-1-66783-527-3

# CHAPTER 1

An unknown virus has spread across the universe. Every living thing across the vast cosmos is living in terror. Over the past few years, people on Earth have experienced a living nightmare. The virus could attack anyone, anything, at any second. Although people have been figuring out a few ways of dodging and surviving the infection, every day brings thousands of new deaths. People have come to understand that only by hiding can they escape this evil force. Living animals and people have been sheltering underground since the virus intensified its violent actions. At this moment, the best scientists in the universe have desperately gathered in the center of space to find the cure.

During the early stages of the virus, a child was born in California. The child was unique. He had beautiful deep black eyes and yet they were somehow transparent like the depths of the Universe. His brown hair also had a radiant sheen. People said he had godly powers because he survived the virus as a toddler. Unlike other unfortunate newborns who died after contracting the virus, this child overcame with great ease the vicious attack of the dominant virus.

The child's name was Hudgus, Chase Hudgus. He wasn't the only child; he had one brother and two sisters. However, his siblings don't have the power Chase has. His father was named James Hudgus, a wealthy businessman, handsome, loyal and respectable. Chase's mother(Jessy) is a gorgeous woman who is a professional chef; she is sweet and loving. His siblings are Ryan, Katrina, and Vitoria. Ryan is a regular 4th grader who is athletic and popular. Katrina is sixteen and plays on the school's volleyball team, and she is pretty smart compared to her classmates. Vitoria is twenty-one and just came back home because of the virus; she is a super-intelligent person that loves studying. Chase was the one of the middle children and he did not get that much attention. However, he did not like attention; in certain ways, Chase enjoyed the freedom of not being the center of attention of his parents. Chase was never a loud person, but the boy was brave and kind-hearted. He was willing to die for his friends and family.

Chase went to a private school in California with his other siblings. Chase got into the smarter class, and he made some friends there. One of them was named Kate and another named David. Kate was brilliant and brave, and she was usually the leader of a group. With Kate having brown hair that smoothly transitions into blonde, and a pair of piercing green eyes. She was a magnificent speaker that could tell stories with tens of thousands of words in the matter of one sentence. And her brilliance in creativity is unmatched. David was a tranquil person, and he didn't like to talk. David was an intelligent person who wanted to build things. Since Chase was a new student, he usually stuck with Kate and David. Fortunately, Kate, David, and Chase were neighbors, so they could talk after school.

A few months went by, and the virus got more serious. More and more people started getting infected. As soon as people noticed the infection became more severe, everyone started to panic. The virus could kill someone instantly and silently, meaning that someone could get the virus without knowing it. When someone got the virus, it often dried out all their blood, making them unconscious and killing them.

Everything shut down, the schools closed, and daily life collapsed. People began to build underground bunkers to prevent the spread of the virus. Fortunately for Chase, his house already had a shelter.

As time went by, people stayed underground for days, and only came to the surface to get food and water. Chase's Bunker was well built with a charming European theme. The Bunker had 2 living rooms, and 8

bedrooms, with 5 restrooms with fantastic heating. And it was also connected to Kate's and David's house. Since Chase was able to see Kate and
David, they were never bored. They played video games together and did
an online class together. After online school is over, they usually research
the virus.

# CHAPTER 2

After a few days, it was Chase's birthday. Chase was turning 15. Chase's birthday party was exceptional because he had David and Kate. Even though no one besides his immediate family and two best friends came to the birthday party, the party was still awesome. Chase's parents bought Chase a huge cake, with balloons, and everyone was happy. Unlike others, they had birthday parties together. Chase was turning 15, and his parents got him and his friends a microscope. Chase didn't really like it at first, but David and Kate used it, so he was happy.

A few days after Chase turned 15, it was David's birthday. David would also be turning 15. David's birthday was similar to Chase's, but Chase and Kate got to know David more. David got a robot model and some anime books in Japanese for his birthday.

"Wait, you can read Japanese?" asked Kate.

"Yeah, I can," responded David.

"How did you learn Japanese?" asked Chase.

"I was born in Tokyo, but I was raised in California," said David.

"How interesting," said Kate.

"David, do you have siblings?" asked Chase.

"No, I am an only child," answered David.

The rest of the birthday went pretty well. David and Chase started to play some video games, and Kate watched them play.

"Wow, you guys are really good at this game. What is the game called by the way?" asked Kate.

"Yep, we have been training every single day," said Chase.

"Oh yeah, the name is Street Fighters," David said.

"Nice, I think we should go study and research for our project," said Kate.

"All right, we have been playing for a few hours," responded Chase.

After they shut off the Playstation XVI, they went to Kate's room to research. They had been trying to find the beginning of the virus. Kate had been asking some scientists about the illness and what was going on.

"Yeah, one of the scientists said that the source of the virus is not from Earth. So the virus might be a universe-wide sickness, or Earth is the only one that has been infected by the virus," said Kate.

"Okay, so if we want to find the cure, we might have to go to outer space? We might get lost and might even not make it back to Earth?!" asked Chase.

"Yeah, probably, because another scientist said by killing the primary source of the virus, the other small sources would die as well," responded Kate.

"Well, how are we supposed to do that?" asked Chase.

"Well, we can design it but we might have to work with the government or build a rocket ourselves. I don't...," David started to explain

"But that might be impossible--" Kate put her hand on David's mouth.

"We WILL find a way," said Kate.

Kate started to look through her laptop for some research while David began designing the rocket. Chase was wondering if there was any possible way that they could work with anyone else except the government and build their own rocket.

"Oh, maybe we can contact Tony Musk," said Chase.

"You mean the best rocket scientist on Earth?" asked Kate.

"Yeah, it would be easier to contact him than the Government," said Chase.

"Well, I guess you are right, but first, we need to design the rocket and make him build it for us," said David.

"Okay," said Chase.

"So I designed the rocket with a large triangular shape, but it doesn't affect the airflow," said David.

"That is great. We can use the robot model you got to test out the design," said Kate.

"Okay," responded David.

Then, David started to create some additional designs and tested out all of them on his computer. One of them was a regular rocket that the government used. Another one was a circular one that looked like a UFO. While David was testing the models, Kate was asking some questions to some scientists. Chase who was writing an email to Tony Musk. Chase wrote:

*Dear Mr. Musk,*

*We are only teenagers but we want to help the Earth during the virus. You might have heard that the primary source of the infection is not from Earth. We believe you are the only one that can help us. We have created some models that might work (see the pictures included).*

*As you can see, we put a lot of effort into this. We would like you to build one of the designs and work with us.*

*Thank You So much*

*Chase Hudgus.*

Kate told Chase to not send the email yet because David didn't know if the rocket worked yet. Chase and Kate were organizing the research while David was still testing the models.

"What did you get from the scientists?" asked Chase.

"One of the scientists said that some of them will form a group to go to space," answered Kate.

"Well, that is some good news, what else?" asked Chase.

"Another scientist said that the center of space is about 200 million light-years away," said Kate.

"Well that is concerning," said Chase.

"No, it is not," answered David.

David shot right up on the chair. David stood right up as if he figured something out.

"I think I got it," shouted David.

"You got what?" asked Chase.

"The model to use in the mission," answered David.

"Which one should we use?" asked Kate.

"We should use the triangular model because it can contain enough engines, and it would have enough space for more than two thousand people. But we still need to simulate the model," said David.

"Then let's do that now," said Chase.

"There is a problem. My pc is not that powerful. We need a super-computer that NASA or the government used," said David

"Maybe we can ask Tony Musk to send a supercomputer,or we should send the model to him to test it," said Kate

"That is an excellent idea," responded Chase.

"I feel like we should send a mini rocket to actually get an idea of what we are dealing with" said Chase

"Yeah, we cannot fight the virus if we don't have an idea of the virus" agreed Kate

"Ok, I suggest that we should drop the sending emails and work on the mini rocket" said David

"Yeah but I am done so let's just send it first and then build the rocket" said Chase

"I will change something and send it to Tony" responded David

So David started to change the email. However, Chase was worried because if Tony Musk did not accept their email, they would never be able to go to space. Chase felt torn but he was starting to think they might have to steal a super-computer from Tony if he didn't agree to work with them. When the fate of all people on Earth was in danger, they needed to get that computer. Chase tried not to think about this possibility of being rejected and prayed that Tony would decide to support the teenagers. Chased made a few changes to his email.

*Dear Mr. Musk,*

*We are only teenagers but we want to help the Earth during the virus and we believe we can with your help. You might have heard that the primary source of the infection is not from Earth. We have created some models that might work as a spaceship to go deep into the center of the Universe. But we need your help to make our designs real.*

*As you can see, we put a lot of effort into this. We would like you to build one of the designs and work with us. We would like to use one of your supercomputers. We would want to test out the*

*models. You could send the computer to us, or we would send the file/model to you.*

*Thank You So much,*

*Chase Hudgus.*

After writing the email, Chase asked Kate and David for an opinion on the email. David said it was good enough, Kate said the email covered most things up, so it had her approval, too. Then, David and Kate started to design and test out the mini rockets. After writing the mail, Chase raced straight to his room. His room was full of books and video games with a cozy small fire. Chase started to construct a drone. Chase wanted to build a drone because they could steal a computer if Tony refused to work with them. Chase worked on it on his own because he didn't know if Tony wanted to work with them.

After a few days, Tony replied to Chase and David. Tony wrote:

*Dear Chase,*

*It is very sweet of you guys to try to help the Earth. Keep trying! Unfortunately, I am very busy and cannot help you, and the government won't allow it. My assistant looked at your designs and ideas and felt they were too risky. I would love to help, but I cannot.*

*Sincerely,*

Tony Musk.

Before they had gotten a response from Tony, the kids had decided to send an unmanned experimental rocket into space; the rocket was 7 feet tall, made all out of Iekruenium, sunstone, and graphene, a super strong material for spacecraft. The rocket's purpose was to gather facts about the virus and allow the kids to go on the next rocket with a better understanding. The rocketship has 10 Canon EOS 6D Mark II Digital SLR Camera Body which is a professional camera made for astrophotography. Each had a

Nikon 800mm lens. Each of the cameras can store 5 PetaByte. The rocket has a speed of 466 thousand miles per second. However, Chase knew Tony would never want to work with them. Chase already had a backup plan. He was already building a drone to steal a super-computer. When Chase broke the news to Kate and David, they were devastated. The conversation went something like this:

"Em guys, Tony kind of declined to work with us," said Chase.

"What! Why?" asked Kate.

"Probably because the government won't let him," answered David.

"And he said his assistant said it was too risky to work with us," added Chase.

"Wow, that hurts," said Kate.

Finally, Chase told them the idea of stealing a computer from Tony. Chase was kind of nervous at first because Kate and David might think he is crazy. Chase was still unsure if he should tell them his plan yet, but later, he decided to tell them the idea.

"About the computers, I have a plan," said Chase.

"Okay, tell us about it," said Kate.

"You know how they deliver the computer with drones," said Chase.

"Okay, what about it?" responded David.

"We can create a drone and try to steal one," said Chase.

"Steal a computer? That is the craziest... What are you thinking?" asked Kate.

"I think it might work," answered Chase.

"Are you crazy! There is no way we can do that!" said Kate.

"Wait, I think it might actually work," said David.

"What? And how?" asked Kate.

"The media has reported that the new super-computers can be transformed into a briefcase-like thing," said David.

"And the computer is metal, which can be dragged by a magnet," added Chase.

"Exactly, so we are not crazy," responded David.

"Whatever, but we don't even know where the computers are?" asked Kate.

"We can track down the location using hacks," said Chase.

"All right let's get to work," shouted David.

Chase showed Kate and David the model of the drone and they said it was doable, but it could be improved. David said it needs to be smaller and more silent because the model that Chase made was quite large and noticeable.

Kate was programming the drone and the controller. While Kate was programming, David was starting to break down the drone. Chase waited. Then, David told Chase that he found a problem but was not ready to reveal the nature of the problem. Kate was close to finishing the program but she could not finish because David was not done building it.

"Done! I basically made a mini version of the old model, but we still need to order something," said David while he was searching through his laptop.

"Yeah, I still need to see the final result before I can finish the program," responded Kate.

"Well, what do we have to order David," asked Chase

"We need some ironsand, a mini camera, and a powerful and silent motor. Since magnets aren't the best for the heist, we need to use ironsand which is a magnet but in sand form, and we need a camera to see what is going on and your motors are weak and loud", answered David.

"WAIT! We need a scout drone to navigate the area" shouted Chase

"Then, just make the drone twice, but the scout drone will have a better camera," answered David.

"And without ironsand, and use the money to get a better camera," said Kate

Later, Chase and David began designing the scout drone and then building it.

Meanwhile, Kate was worrying about the next step of their mission: the rocket flight to the center of the Universe. Was it not very probable that David, Chase and she might not even make it back alive. The mission could be a total disaster. The boys were too caught up in the thrill of building to calmly measure their real chances of survival. It would be her job to bring reality back into the equation. Kate tried to get a hold of her fears. She did believe that the technology that they had was remarkably better than others.

"There, we have the model and the base ready!" announced Chase.

"All we need is to order a camera and motors," added David.

"Well, let's ask our parents to buy it for us, or use our own allowance," said Kate.

Then, David and Chase went into the bunker's lobby to find their parents who were watching TV.

"Hi, mom! Hi, Dad!" said Chase.

"Hello!" answered Chase's mom.

"Hi, son," replied Chase's Dad.

"I was wondering if you guys can buy us something since it is for a project," asked Chase.

"Well, we need to know what you guys are working on," answered Chase's Dad.

"Oh, we are trying to build a drone that can fly long-range and with a clear view over the computers," explained Chase.

"What for?" asked Chase's mom.

"Just for fun and for learning about engineering" answered Chase.

"Okay, what do you need to buy?" asked Chase's Dad.

"We need two cameras, some ironsand, and four motors," said David.

"Alright, I will order that for you boys right now," said Chase's mom.

After saying goodbye to Chase's parents, Chase and David went downstairs to their gaming center. The gaming center had two professional computers, two gaming consoles, a tv, and a room full of snacks. Chase and David started playing GTA XVII, and Call of Duty LVI. The boys forgot about Kate. In some way, Chase and David did not care because they were so tired and needed a break. While the boys were gaming, Kate was still working on the programming because she was concerned that things wouldn't go as well as they expected. Kate didn't want anything to go wrong. Then, Chase and David went to see Kate.

"You good, Kate?" asked Chase

"Yeah, I am fine," answered Kate.

"Most people say when a girl says they are fine, they are not fine," added David.

"I am just worried that things might not go as we expect," answered Kate.

"Well, it is going to be fine," said Chase.

"Well, I guess it's good to look up," said Kate.

"Yeah, let's go eat dinner," said David.

Then, Chase, David and Kate all went to the living room to eat dinner. Chase was ravenous because he hadn't had snacks or lunch. David was also ravenous because he was busy gaming but he expressed it as "used too much brain power." Kate was not really having a good day and didn't really want to eat. However, David's mom said food wouldn't be served before 7 o'clock. Chase and David had to wait two more hours until dinner. While waiting Chase and David went back to gaming, and Kate helped her mom clean the shelter.

"Oh my god, we still have to wait two more hours until dinner! Maybe we will eat some snacks and drink some G Fuel," said David.

"Nah, the chef said he is making something big and ambrosial tonight. Maybe drink some water or eat some nuts," answered Chase.

"Alright, let's just play a little bit more," suggested David.

"Sure, but make sure to keep a timer. We don't wanna miss dinner," answered Chase.

The boys started gaming again while Kate was cleaning the shelter. Kate started to clean her room first and went from her room to the dining room.

"Man, we have so many more rooms to clean," said Kate.

"But we still have tomorrow," said Kate's mom.

"I guess so," answered Kate.

Then, Kate went to the kitchen to help the chef prepare dinner. Kate asked the chef what they were having. The chef said, "lobsters and oyster."

"Tonight is special because it has been exactly two years since quarantine began," the chef said.

"For me, it is not a very nice day to celebrate, but I guess this doesn't happen every year. And I also love lobster," said Kate.

Then, Kate left the kitchen suddenly, without being noticed. Since Kate left in a big hurry, the parents who were in the living room thought something was up with her. Then, Kate started to run toward her room. The parent thought she felt anxiety; sweat and fear started to overpower her. She slammed and locked the door. The parents didn't mind this at first, but Kate did not show up to eat dinner, which was surprising because she told the chef she was excited. Five minutes into dinner, Kate still hadn't shown up, yet her parents continued not to worry; they assumed she had just forgotten. Fifteen minutes, and still no Kate. At this point, her parents grew concerned and asked Chase or David to check on her. David went and did not come back to dinner. Then Chase went to check on David and Kate, and he also did not return.

After dinner, the parents realized that something was not right. David's mom went to Kate's room and found out that the group of kids were immersed in research. Apparently they had sunk so deeply into their project, they had completely forgotten about dinner.

The parents were still confused because why would Kate nervously run into her room. Kate just responded that she didn't want to forget her thoughts and ideas and she wasn't nervous at all, they just didn't see her face.

While they were researching the virus.......

By this time, their mini rocket had gone 50 million lightyears and sent back vital information. The mini rocket had found out that it wasn't really a virus. Surprisingly, humans can't give the virus to each other. The virus, like a killer who wants to eliminate one specific person, chases after individuals. But the virus does not feel satisfied with one victim but instead, like a serial killer, enjoys multiple slayings. And like a mob boss, this deadly virus allows his smaller and less powerful servants to do the killing.

To defeat the virus is to find the primary source and destroy it. Technically, it means that even if Earth managed to defeat the virus on Earth, it could still come back to Earth. The central goal was to defeat the virus once and for all. After they researched, they went to sleep for the night.

The next day, it was pouring rain outside. The package they ordered arrived at 5:00 am. They couldn't get their hands on the package until 12:00 pm. The package went through the regular cleaning, which involved 12 times of germs X-ray, 12 times UV-light cleaning, 36 times bleach spray, and finally wiping everything with alcohol. When Chase, David and Kate FINALLY got the package, they started assembling the parts to the drone. Chase and David worked on assembling the drone, while Kate added some final lines of code to the program. After they assembled the final parts, they could not do a test run outside but they could do a test run in their almost built indoor Basketball court. The test flight was very impressive, the motors and the flying were good, but the ironsand and the container did not open as well as the motor.

"Oh my God, the ironsand is spilling everywhere. Quick, someone fix the container. If we can get it back, this will only be a slight delay," said David.

"Okay, okay, you can depend on me," said Chase.

The kids stopped working for that day because it was already dark after the test flight. They weren't that disappointed but they were pretty sad. The next day, the kids went back to fixing the drone after they had eggs and bacon. They cooked the food themselves because he needed a healthy diet in order to be an astronaut and they did not want their parents to know their plan. After they ate breakfast, they went straight back to fixing the drone. Kate and Chase started fixing the drone, while David was checking the program. Even though they were confused they still figured the problem out. The problem was that the container and the ironsand were not fitable for Kate's program. After David made the code fitable for the done, they went to test flight again. The worst possible result they can get is that the drone doesn't function and explodes. Well, it went the opposite of that, and the drone and pick up and the flying was improved, quieter and quicker.

"Yess, that was sooo easy" said David

"Well, maybe the coding part was easy, but fixing the drone was sooo hard" said Kate

"Well, we can finally fly the drone and steal a computer now," said Chase

"We should do that tomorrow, because it is lunch and me and Chase have to practice basketball" said David

"Oh yeah, I forgot about that," said Chase

Then, Kate went back inside to rest while the boys went to the locker room and changed into their jerseys. After they changed, they went to the basketball court and practiced some shots. Chase was a small forward, while David was a point guard. Chase chose to be a small forward because he has size and he is athletic. On the other hand, David isn't that big and he doesn't like to be bumped and fouled. At first Chase was guarding David, and David was almost always behind the three point line. On the other hand, David guarded Chase, and Chase was almost always under the basket or dunking. After they practiced, they went to eat lunch. Chase and David had sandwiches, while Kate had salads. After lunch, the kids got a brief location of the computers, and sent the scout drone to get a closer look at the surroundings. After the launch, Chase and David went to gaming for a break. While Kate went to talk to her other friends online. The next day, the drone arrived near the location. After the drone arrived at the location, Chase took control of the drone.

"Whoa, this place is very secured, I think we should attach some protection on the drone," said Chase

"The idea is right but what should we add?" asked David

"Maybe some sleeping darts that can make people fall asleep. We are not harming them." suggested Kate

"Well, let's just scout the surroundings" said Chase

After they got a better view of the surroundings, the drone went into the building through an air tunnel, which led to the worker sections.

"Oh shoot, there is a lot of people in this room, we shouldn't be here" said Kate

"Yeah, I'll fly back to the air tunnel." said Chase

Some workers were kind of suspicious of the drone, but they didn't know what it was so they let it go. The drone kept going, they went into Tony Musk's office.

"I have heard that you need to go through his office to the super-computers" said David

"Well, we probably need a locksmith to open the door." said Chase

"We could just add a laser to open the door" said David

"I think we should send the drone back, because we don't want any risks" said Kate

After the drone went out of the building, some people spotted the drone. Suddenly the alarm went off. The workers have spotted the drone, they started to send other drones to bring down the drone. However, they were not fast enough, they were made for defending, while the kids' drones were made for scouting and being fast. The drones kept chasing until dawn. The company's had an advantage at first because they knew the environment well, however later outside of the company's area the kids had an advantage.

Then, the company's drone started rapidly shooting BB bullets. The kids' drones were almost brought down; one of the wings was damaged severely. However, the other parts of the drone were not damaged. The enemy drone lost track after the kids' drone went into the forest near their house. Some of the company's drones kept chasing while most just stopped. Since the kids knew the place well, they juked some of the company's drones and made them crash onto the tree.

"Wow, that was a close call." said Chase

"At least we know the surroundings and the inside of the building," said Kate.

Then, they heard the news in the living room. The news said: *"A mysterious drone was seen near Tony Musk's company. If anyone knows any more info please contact Tony's company. If anyone knows where the drone is, they will be rewarded 1,000 dollary doos."*

"Wow, the world is crazy these few years: the virus, riots, and now drones flying around," said Chase's mom in a surprised voice.

"Yeah, and it was also last seen right next to our forest," said David's mom.

After the kids heard that, they went straight back to the research room.

"Did you guys hear that?! We are wanted!" whispered Kate.

"No one's gonna know; we brought the drone in on time," said David as he assured Kate.

"But we should be careful. They last saw the drone in the forest next to us. But it is ok, we should be fine," added Chase.

After the conversation, each of them went to bed. The next day, some police came to the forest and investigated. Then, one of the police came and asked the family if they had seen the drone. Most of them said no, while

Chase's brother, Ryan, said that he heard some noises in the forest. The police said that they are already investigating it. Chase, David, and Kate were not worried at all. The police didn't even care about what they said. It was a surprise that the police didn't even come check the house before they left.

"Wow, that was kind of a close call, even though the police didn't come in and check," said Kate.

"Yeah, but we should still be careful," responded Chase.

"I thought your brother was going to give us away," said David.

"Well, at least he didn't," said Chase.

The kids did not work on the project for 3 weeks. The police were investigating for 2 weeks, but some people came and looked for the drone. During the investigation, Chase, David, and Kate were adding some accessories in order to open the door to the computers. On the scout drone, David suggested that they should add some sleeping darts in order to create time for the big drone to open the door. Chase really liked that idea. So Chase ordered a dart shooting darts turret, it is like a paintball turret but for darts, and some one hour sleep darts. They also order a Spyder IV, the strongest handheld laser. While they were waiting, Kate created a button punching machine that would press the button when needed. Chase, David, and Kate were sharing allowances that their parents gave them each week. Also, doing chores would also earn them money.

"Wow, that was almost over the budget of our allowance," said Chase.

"We can't buy anything until next month, yay!" said David.

"At least we can finally get this done with," responded Kate.

After a few weeks, Chase, David, and Kate earned more money. The parts that they needed also came in the mail in the morning. Of course it went through the usual cleaning. The next day, the kids got their hands on it and started working. Chase was trying to work the turret and the dart out, while David was creating a space for the turret. Kate was trying to put the laser on the button punch that David made. The process was slow, however, and they finished the building by the evening.

There was a problem; that the workers in the company will be much safer next time. It will be troublesome to go into the building and complete the heist. However, David said that by the time they try to complete the heist, the heavily guarded builded will not be heavily guarded. Kate guessed that the next time they sent the drone that would not be anytime soon. They went to sleep for the night and woke up the next morning to find the drone had gone missing.

"Oh my gosh, where is the drone?" asked Kate

"I don't know, David was suppose to put it away," answered Chase

"Well, I put the drone right here," said David as he pointed toward the spot.

Instantly, they stopped talking and started to look for the drone. David was checking his room, Chase was searching in his own room and Kate's room. While the boys were searching the rooms, Kate was searching in the living room and the kitchen. They kept looking until the afternoon; David checked and the drone was not there. Chase searched his and Kate's room and found nothing. They kept searching for the next 5 days and still found nothing. After a few days, they still had no idea where the drone was. However, they did know where the drone was last seen. After more days of searching, they finally found the drone. Chase's brother took their drone. His brother gave it back, but they didn't know why he took it in the first place. It had been exactly 3 weeks and 6 days since the scout drone went out.

"We finally found the drone after almost a week" said David

"We should have asked your brother in the first place," said Kate.

"At least we got the drone back" said Chase

Right after they got the drone back, they started working. They already finished the building part so they worked on the coding part. Kate was coding the laser while Chase and David worked on the dart turret. It was fairly difficult to code the turret because they had to work in the shooting, turning, and the aiming. However, after Kate finished her job, which was to aim, and click the button, she went to help the boys, they did not finish until the next afternoon.

After they finished, they launched it immediately. As David thought, the security was not as closely guarded as 2 weeks ago. After 5 minutes, the drone found the way in the tall, black building. The original spot was closed by the company. The drone was confused at first because it had a totally different environment, but it did find the way. However, Chase, David, and Kate did not think that there were drones inside the company's building guarding the inside. Instantly, when they entered the first room, one of the guardian drones spotted their drone. As soon as they were spotted, the guardian told every other drone to come and attack their drone. A second later, the alarm went off. David flew the drone right outside of the building. Seeing almost 20 drones surrounding the building. Instantly, David zoomed out of the building. Other drones spotted their drone, but couldn't catch up. Their drone was accelerating at 56 miles per hour, catching a top speed of 150 miles per hour. The guardian drones were heavily armed with iron and BB bullets. Instantly, the guardian drones sent the chase drones to chase down their drone and destroy the drone. The chase drone was lightly armed with a small amount of BB bullets, but it was insanely fast. Accelerating 78 miles per hour, at a top speed of 205 miles per hour. However, it can be easily destroyed. At the beginning of the chase the chase drones had an advantage, because the chasing drone knew the surroundings better, and it was a lot faster. After a few turns in the city, it was out of the chasing drones range. The chasing drones didn't know the surroundings well, and some crashed into buildings and breaking glass since it was going at such a high speed. Then, a lot of the drones just stopped and went back to their center. Then, in the evening, the drone finally returned to the bunker. After they got the drone back, they knew the building well. They thought they would just wait for 2 weeks and send both drones. After considering that drones are probably going to chase them again. David suggested that the drone needs some kind of weapon to attack other drones. Chase thought about it and suggested that BB bullets are the best choice.

"I think BB bullets are the best choice," said Chase.

"Don't you think that the drones are BB bullet proof since they have armor?" asked Kate.

"Yeah, we should make or buy something stronger" said David

"We should make the bullets heavier and make the shooting machine more powerful," said Kate.

"Well, first of all we need more turrets," said David.

"We don't have one already, we can just switch bullets," said Chase.

"That is going to be harder to code, but it is not impossible," said Kate.

"Then, we can do it. I ain't trying to waste money and our parents will get suspicious of us just buying random things." said Chase

Later, David and Kate started to invent a more powerful BB bullet that can go through basic BB bullet armor. They added 0.5 ounce of wurtzite boron nitride and tungsten for the shells of the bullet. The total purchase is about 500 dollars. Even though it was very expensive, they wanted to help Earth. So money wasn't that important compared to the whole human race. After a few days, the news talked about the drone incident again. The reporter said "Drones were seen at the Musk's industry, if any caught the predator, they would be rewarded ten thousand bitcoins, and the predator would be sentenced for life in ADX Florence.

"Oh my god, did you hear that? We will be put into the highest security prison for life " whispered Kate.

"I know but they are probably not going to find out" said David

"Even if they find out, we would just tell them the cause and he would be fine." added Chase

After the conversation, Chase and David said goodbye and went to play some games. The boys didn't seem that worried, however, Kate was still concerned. However, Kate still let it go. After a few days, the news reported another news that they found the drone and the owner. The kids found it confusing because they weren't caught yet. The police or anyone didn't even come to their house. At least now they wouldn't have to go to prison for the rest of their lives.

"I wonder who they captured, at least we are clear" said Kate

"I feel bad for the guy that was captured," said Chase.

"The guy did it for a good cause, so at least not everything is wrong," said David.

After a few days the material for the bullets arrived. As usual it went through the cleaning. And the kids received the package in the afternoon. David and Chase went to create the new bullet straight away. However, the kids do not know what the guardian drones' using for armor. What the kids knew was that the guardian drone is slow. Kate suggests that they would use their mediocre speed as an advantage. There is a slight problem, the rooms aren't that big, it is easier for the guardian drones to shoot them down before they can fly around and dodge the bullets. The kids had lots of disadvantages, which makes the mission very difficult to pull off. The kids realized that they had to use their advantage to the fullest.

"Wow, we have a hard mission to pull off, I just realized that" said David

"That is why we have to use our advantage to the fullest, and that is why we are taking so long so prepare" answered Kate

"You know sometimes I think about quitting the mission, but we already started the mission" said Chase.

During the conversation, somewhere in the galaxy the virus became more intensified. The virus started acting more active than ever. The virus became so intensified that even talking and staring at someone that had the virus on the other side of the world could get the virus. Since the virus became more dangerous the whole cosmos stated that the virus was a lion level danger; which means their cosmos could be wiped out. There were 5 danger levels, first being the rhino level; which means a planet was at risk. Second, being the tiger level; which means a system of planets is at risk. Thirdly, the snake level; it means that a whole galaxy can be wiped off of existence. Fourthly, the lion level; which means that a whole cosmos can get wiped out. Lastly, the DRAGON level; which means that literally EVERYTHING will be designated to be wiped out. Chase's universe is on the fourth level, and the top scientists predict that the virus will evolve and become a DRAGON level danger. Five days went by and they finally finished the bullets. Even though they finished creating the bullets, they still needed to change the turret a little more. However, the turret's muzzle is too big for the BB bullets.

"The muzzle is too big for our bullets," said David.

"What should we do?" asked Chase

"I don't know if we can buy another turret, but as you said we should save money," responded David.

"Is there any other choice?" asked Chase

"I don't think so, but we could just not use the bullets," said Kate.

"No, we have to use the bullets; we already spent time on it, and it is necessary" said Chase

"OK, that we have to buy another turret" said David

After the conversation, Chase went on Yamazon and bought a turret that fits perfectly with the bullet. 4 days later, the turret came in the mail. After they got it, they instantly inserted the turret on top of the drone and 3d printed a box connected to the turret. Later Kate and Chase started programming the turret. They got it done the next afternoon. After they got it done, they went into their indoor basketball court and tested it out. The drone acted well, and the aim of the turrets was pretty good and consistent. To truly test out, the kids created an obstacle course. There were dart boards, and BB bullet targets. While shooting the targets, they also have to move along, and dodge other BB bullets. Sometimes Chase has to take over the computer and fly the drone. So Chase had 4 days to make his flying skills better.

The first day, Chase crashed a lot and missed a lot of targets, however Chase is kind of getting the hang of the controls. The second day, Chase improved a little. The aim was a lot better, but the flying wasn't as good as the aim. The third day, Chase's aim improved a little, while he really improved in flying. The final day, every section of shooting and flying, Chase managed to do a pretty good job in 4 days. Chase can do it well enough that they can at least get the computer. The next day, they sent the drone, the different thing is that they sprayed some forest camouflage on. Since the building is near the forest, it gives them another small advantage. By the time they reached the building, it was almost evening. The workers are about to go home. This is also an advantage because people won't be there. However, the disadvantage is that there would be more drones and automatic remote control cars. Which means it will be easy inside the building, but it will be much harder outside. As soon as they got about 50 meters near the building, there were already 5 drones guarding. The mission is going to be harder to execute because not only the scout drone that is going, the main drone is also coming. Later, the scouting drone went ahead out of the forest and near the building.

Then, Chase took over the control and went around the building. Chase noticed that the guardian drones have a pattern of movement. The guardian drones seemed to have a rule, one moves then another moves. Chase noticed and waited for 5 minutes to check if this rule applies to every drone. This pattern can create a huge disadvantage for Chase to fly around. However, this pattern can also create a huge advantage for Chase. Chase still waited to test something out. The scouting drone shot a BB bullet at a branch. As the branch fell, every guardian drone seemed to notice and rushed to the branch. Chase understood that if one thing happens every drone will go check it out. This would create a huge gap for Chase to enter the building. Chase called for the stealing drone, when the stealing drone was next to the scout drone. Chase shot five bullets to five branches. As the branches fell, drones rushed to every branch. As the guardian drones checked the branch out. The scouting and the stealing drones rushed to the nearest air tunnel. As the stream of air went beside some of the guardian drones. The drones were totally baffled, and alerted. Chase has a very difficult time, trying to balance and not crash into one of the air tunnel's walls. Chase also has to slow down time and time, because their drones will make a little bit of noise, and the air tunnel makes it louder and spreads the noise around the building. After a few minutes flying around the building, they found the air entrance to Tony Musk's office. Chase went through the entrance. The scout drone went in first, the stealing drone entered when the scouting drone gave it a signal. Once they entered, the stealing drone went straight to cutting the security door to the super computers instantly. While the stealing drone was cutting, the scouting drone was flying right in front of the door and guarding the stealing drone.

The noise that the bullets created is kind of loud, and it gets a lot of attention. While cutting, some of the drones heard the noise and went straight to the boss's office. However, Chase was ready. Once the drone 'stepped' onto the boss's ground, Chase lasered BB bullets at its head. Even though it made some sound, one guardian drone was down. By the time, the defeated guardian drone fell onto the ground; other guardian drones had already noticed the defeated drone. When Chase noticed, he zoomed right out of the business man's office. Leaving the thief drone alone, Chase did it on purpose because he wanted the guardian drones to chase him instead of destroying the defenseless stealing drone. However, some of the drones chased him while two other drones went to check the office. Chase instantly noticed that and quickly turned and shot at the two drones. One was brought down, but the other was not. Then, David took control of the stealing drone and shot out a laser beam. Even though the drone was not brought down, it was knocked out. Now that the stealing was safe, Chase flew around the lobby and shot some drones down. At one point, the turret for the bullets was stuck. It could not operate and shoot. Chase couldn't do anything but fly around.

However, thinking on his feet, Chase purposely crashed into a few drones--knocking a few of them down. While Chase took care of the guardian drones, David was cutting the entrance to the supercomputers. David was being thoughtful and used some of his time to cut a hole through the wall, in case of emergency they can just go through the hole that leads to the outside. Half way through the cutting, it was 4 A.M. Chase was worried that they wouldn't have enough time before the workers came to work. David sped up the cutting by getting closer to the metal door.

While the boys were controlling the drone, Kate was doing extra research. What she found was surprising, even though she knew that light could technically move objects; which is solar sails. She didn't know that it could be used for actual movement. As Kate being genius as she is, she hoped to implant a little bit of reflecting foil that acts like a wing. So that if they run out of power(which won't happen) they can use the light to move. Now that they won't run out of power, she is more hopeful.

Now back to Chase and David, David finally cut open the door and went into the vault for the supercomputers. While David was in the vault searching for the computers, Chase was still battling the guardian drones. A lot of them had already crashed but there was one more drone. The only drone left was more powerful than the others, it's like it was Darth Vader, while the others were the Stormtroopers. There were exactly two drones left. The turret was back to normal, and Chase was able to shoot again. David found the supercomputers, and was amazed how advanced technology had become; that it can communicate with the government and companies has greater technology but people just don't know.

While thinking, the stealing drone picked up the suitcase supercomputer. And told Chase that as he got the computers. When Chase heard that, he still flew around and shot. Giving David time to fly away, since it is not that fast. When David was two miles away from the building. Chase zoomed out of the building. Reaching a new top speed of 298 miles per hour. Of course, the Chasing drones were released. Chase decided to distract the chasing drones, and crash into them to bring them down. Chase eventually brought down five of them at the same time. Later, Chase shot and crashed into the drones. When there were no drones left, Chase kept flying. However, the scouting drone was heavily damaged. Two third of the route back home, the scouting drone crashed onto a tree and was brought down. Chase finally lost control and had to watch David make it home safely. Later, the stealing drone made it home and brought back the supercomputer. David and Kate went to sleep for the rest of the night. However, Chase had some trouble sleeping. So he woke up and started messing with the supercomputer. On the black, unnoticeable computer, there was a finger sized silver button. Chase was skeptical of the button. He thinks it would trigger some kind of alarm. However, after a few minutes of messing with the computer. Chase decided to press the button. The button didn't trigger any alarm, but it expanded into a laptop. However, they have the computer on, but they don't have access to the computer. They don't have the password to the computer. He was devastated, they have dones so much to get the computer but still cannot use the computer. Chase felt hopeless, and he had nothing to do, so he went to sleep. However, Chase had a plan.

The next morning, David woke up first and opened the computer. Same as the result Chase got, they don't have the password. Unlike Chase, David went to check the footage the stealing drone got. Later, Kate woke up and found David dumbfounded.

"What happened, something wrong?" asked Kate

"YES, everything is wrong," answered David.

"What happened," asked Kate

"First, we done know the password the stupid computer; why wouldn't a computer have a passowrd. Second, my stupid bed collapsed in the middle of the *frickin* night," answered David angrily.

"WHAT, we don't have the password." said Kate

"Yes, in fact we didn't even think about the computer having a password in the first place" said David

"First of all, calm down. We will find the password" said Kate calmly.

"How are we supposed to do that, go there again like nothing happened," asked David

"Woah, guys chill. It is only 9 o'clock in the morning," Chase enter the room and said

"What about the password" said David

"I know, I checked the computer out yesterday at night" said Chase

"What do we do then?" asked David.

"Have you checked the footage that we have" asked Chase

"In fact, I have" said David

"Good, have you seen any weird signs" asked Chase

"Well, no much just a bunch of small letters on the some of the computers" answered David

"Put those letters together, and type it on the computer," said Chase.

*A few seconds later.*

"I did, and it didn't work, we need a five letter password, this is only four" said David.

"Well, what do the four letters spell out?" asked Chase.

"Uskm, skmu, Oh musk" answered Kate

"Well, the last letter should be?" asked Chase

"S, Musks" shouted David.

Then, David excitedly put in the code.

"Yessssss, it WORKED" said David

After knowing the code, David knew exactly what to do. He opened the SLS LX, which is a rocket testing program. And put in a usb that contained the models and the program then started generating. They left the room and went to get lunch because it would take quite a long time to complete all the models. While they were taking a break. The news broke out that a heist was practiced at the Tony's company main building. The news reporter said it was a kind of an attack, since a part of a wall was torn apart. The inside of the building was smally damaged, but Tony's office was damaged severely. The police have stated "The incidents of drone attacks have been consistent, we will try our best to find the drone owner, for now we will release the person that was involved in these series of attacks". After half an hour, one of the models was completed.

"The first one was completed" said Chase

"I think we should wait until all of them finishes" said Kate

"Yeah, it is able to handle all to them at the same time, but it will slow down the process" said David

As they waited, the virus came closer and closer to Earth. Meanwhile, terrorizing each and every planet it passed by. The creature that has met or even caught the virus has said sometimes it will control your mind into crazy and evil thoughts. Shortly, after having thoughts of evil, a black figure would appear and stare at you. Only the people who contracted the virus would figure while others could not. The terrifying and weird fact is that the information could not be spread. The communication between planets would not work. Electronic mail would not be delivered. While actual mail would get destroyed or would disappear. Even if you know some information, the person would simply disappear or be found dead. Scientists have noticed the virus is acting more like a living creature.

A few minutes passed by, the program completed and ran all the models. Once it finished, David went into the room and saw the results of the models.

The first model, which was the primitive model of all. The benefits were that it was the most aerodynamic; that will reduce drag which is a very important aspect due to the speed that the rocket will be traveling at. Body of the rocket will be difficult to create because they have to be concerned about the flow velocity, pressure, density, and temperature. The advantage of the model is that the rocket would reduce drag and reduce force from air. As Newton's Third Law states that for every action, there is an equal and opposite reaction. This model reduces the opposite force. The force is still there but the rocket is going through it. This model is the opposite of being outmoded but, popular two hundred years ago, but it is still popular right now.

The second model has the simulate of the first one. The second one is a large, triangular shape. The main attraction of the model is the massive engine and the storage of the rocket. The massive energy and speed the rocket can produce is more than impressive. The second rocket is purely made of being fast and aerodynamic. The velocity of this speed demon is beyond imaginable. The downfall of the speed demon is the problem: it is toil and rigor to slow down. The speed demon is a beast but it is not quite controllable.

While the first two models are completely different from the third one, it doesn't mean it won't do the same job as the first two. The material of the engine is made of elaeolite. A purple gemstone found in the deep Arctic of Earth III. This gemstone could generate a huge amount of power when heated. If the gemstone is connected to the engine, the rocket could blast off. The model is like a plane. It is easy to control, and it is easy to build. Except the gemstone is difficult to get. However, Chase's dad has a huge company, and it has a reasonable source of workers at Earth III. That would make it easier, but it is still incredibly difficult to get.

After David got a brief look at the results and was actually surprised. The models actually did reasonably well. The models all have problems, but it is a small problem. The main problem is the building materials. Otherwise they are ready to go. Even though the rocket is pretty much ready, they still don't know where to go. They can't just ramble around the universe. Later, David told Kate and Chase the result.

"Wow, we succeeded," said Chase.

"Except we still have to build it," said David.

"At least the programming and the design didn't have any trouble," said Kate.

# CHAPTER 3

The light appeared in the middle of darkness. Chase found himself a few meters away from the ball of light. The light turned yellow, like the light was reading Chase's expression.

"Woah, where am I," said Chase

The ball of light turned green, and I was making musical notes.

"What was that," said Chase as he tried to touch the ball of light.

The ball of light dodged back. It turned into another shape. It struggled a bit, and Chase was confused about what the light was going to do. A few seconds later, the light turned into the shape of a human.

"Hello," said the white figure.

"Hello, who are you," said Chase.

"Doesn't matter, I am in a hurry," said the figure.

"So you know about the incidents that have been killing millions right?" said the Figure

"Yes, but isn't the criminal caught?" said Chase

"Yes, but do you think the case is that simple? In the next few days you are going to see more and more criminal activity and supernatural incidents," said the figure.

"Ok, why does it matter?" said Chase.

"It matters because if we don't destroy the main cause of these various incidents, the incidents will keep happening," said the figure.

"How do you know that, it is not like it has happened in the past," said Chase.

"No, these incidents have happened in the past, the space center has just covered it up," said the figure.

"Give me an example, if you know about any of them," asked Chase.

"The Mystery of the Raining Meat, The Ships in the Sky; back in 218 B.C, the Jose Bonilla Observation, The Voynich Manuscript, and many more," said the figure.

"That doesn't prove anything. You are just saying random Alien sightings and some weird writing that no one understands," said Chase.

"Listen to me, these groups of people have been watching the entire universe since the beginning of time!" said the Figure.

"What is wrong with watching other planets, and observing what is happening on other planets," said Chase.

"Hey, my time is very tight. The point that I am trying to tell you is; what is out there can possibly destroy the whole universe. We need to get help to stop it," said the Figure

As the figure finished his sentence, it vanished and Chase woke up full of sweat. He was light headed at the moment. With so many questions unanswered in his head.

As he got up from his bed, he noticed a strange book that was not supposed to be there. Chase stood up, walked toward the table. The book had a weird design on the cover. Chase turned to the first page and nothing was there. As Chase sat there for 10 minutes and finally found a page with something written on it. It said "*The group of maraud'r has't did exist as longeth as the beginning of timeth. The square is inescapable, thee cannot defeat the foe. Needeth m're pow'r. Allies. Knowledge, and holp from all* ". Chase balked for a few seconds, and understood what it meant. It meant "The group of killers have been existing from the beginning of time. The fight is inescapable, you cannot defeat the opponent. Need more power, allies, knowledge and help from all."

Chase didn't understand what the person meant by the fight. But everything else was pretty easy to understand.

The other mystery was who was the one who wrote this and is on Chase's table. After sinking into more and more confusion. Chase got out of bed and finished his morning routine. He carried the notebook into the hallway. Chase marched slowly and heavily toward Kate's room. Once he arrived at his destination, Chase knocked on the wooden door.

"Hey, Kate, are you awake yet?" yelled Chase

"Yeah I am, wassup," said Kate,

"I have a few questions," said Chase.

"Sure!" said Kate

As she made the gesture for Chase to come into her room.

When Chase entered, he was greeted with a heavy scent of roses and flowers. Chase really didn't like the smell. He didn't make any action or noise to suggest that he didn't like it, since he didn't want to be rude.

"Um, do you know anything about this note?" asked Chase

As he held up the notebook.

"No, why?" answered Kate.

"I found this on my table in the morning," said Chase.

"Well, does it have anything in?" asked Kate

"Yes, there was a line of quotes, and a page of random dots and dashes," said Chase,

"A page of dots?" asked Kate

"Yes, a page of dots. Let me just show you," responded Chase as he pulled out the notebook. And turned to the last page.

"What does it mean?"

"-.... / ..- -. ... - --- .--. .--. .- -... .-.. / -- ..- ... - / -.... / ... - ---- .--. .--.
. -.. .-.-.- / - .... / ..- -. ... --- . .-. ... . / .-- .. .-.. .-.. / -.... / - -.. ... - -.-.
--- -.-- . -.. .-.-.- / .... . -. -.. / .... . .-. .-. .-.-.- / .... . -. -.. / .... . .-.. .-.-.
-.-.-- / .-- . / -.. --- -. .----. - / .... .- ... . / -- ..- -.-. .... / - .. -- . / .-.. .
..-. - .-.-.- / ..--- ----- -..-. ----- ---.. -..-. -... ----- ----.---.."

"I don't know, it might be morse code or a interuniversal code." said Kate

"Well, anyway I am going to ask David about this," said Chase,

"Okay, I guess see you at breakfast," responded Kate.

Chase walked out of the room carefully as he didn't want to knock Kate's shelf of books down. As soon as he got out, Chase breathed in a ton of "fresh" oxygen. And walked lightly along the hallway of the underground 2nd floor. As Chase slowly progressed toward David's door, the smell of burnt paper became heavier and heavier. Once Chase finally arrived at his destination, the smell was so bad that it seemed like there was an explosion.

*Knock, Knock.*

"David, you alright in there?" asked Chase confusingly

"Ahem. Ahem, yeah I am fine. You can come in if you want," said David.

Chase slowly reached for the door handle. As Chase started to turn the handle, the door swung open. David standing right in front of Chase. Chase noticed something different. Something drastically different.

Before Chase could ask, another object caught his eyes. Quickly, Chase put his attention back on David. David, who was not in good condition, grabbed Chase's arm and pulled him into his own room. David's lab coat was half burnt, and his hairstyle completely changed overnight. Last morning his hairstyle was still wavey, however this morning it became an afro.

"What happened to you?" asked Chase

"Experimental accident, which happens quite often." answered David.

"Okay, anyway. Do you know anything about this note?" asked Chase as he raised the notebook.

David squinted his eyes to get a better look of it. David's expression was really diaphanous at the moment. He was never like that.

"No, the dots and dashes are really confusing. Not sure what it means." said David

"Yeah, I just found this on my table this morning." said Chase

"Well, that is kind of weird. Anyways, I am going to clean up my blown up room. See you at breakfast," said David.

Chase stepped out as he was still studying the code. Chase started to wander around the hallway, trying to get the meaning of the code. He walked and tried to walk back to his room to do some research. However, something caught his ear. Some of the adults were talking about last night? Chase found the conversation hard to hear. He walked closer to the wall, close enough where his body quietly slammed onto the wall. Chase heard "Last", "Night", "Strange", "Figure", "Footsteps" and ".....Door". After trying to connect the words together, Chase was sure something was up last night. Something strange happened, that something might just have left the note for him.

# CHAPTER 4

Chase quickly moved back to his room. As soon as Chase entered his room, his phone started to get notifications like crazy. Usually Chase never gets this amount of notification. Chase shakingly grabbed his phone. Pull downed the notification center. Chase's expression changed drastically. He felt confused and apprehensive. Most of the notifications were news.

*"Weird Light Seen Near Central Forest! And Left With an Unknown Note??"*

*"Unknown Trail In the Sky Near Central Forest! And Mysterious Note?'*

*"Visitors Seen A Light Figure Near Central Forest Area!"*

*"New Alien Sighting??"*

Chase dropped his phone. Staring at the air where trepidation and dreadfulness fills the entire room. Chase quickly brought himself together after all of the thoughts he had. Chase later went out of his room to have breakfast. On the way to the dining room, he went to check David and his room. Chase knocked on David's door, no one answered. Chase knocked again and no one answered. Chase opened the wooden door, and was amazed and somewhat surprised and confused. Everything was cleaned and new. The smell and the color of the burning were all gone. It seemed like he was in a new room with new furniture fresh from IEKA. The odd thing is there were wheel traces on the dusted wooded ground. And a weird screeching noise is heard in the bathroom. As Chase opened the door leading to the bathroom and saw a few dozen car type minion robots, moving around vacuuming and cleaning the tiles of David's floor.

"Ahhhhh! Hide Minions! Hide!" said one of the robots as the expression on the windshield clearly changed. The army of car robots drove around and some hid in the cabinets. Chase was still in shock and muddled.

"Hey, I am David's friend. I am Chase. I will not do any harm." responded Chase.

None of the cars listened. They continued zooming around, and some drove out of the Bathroom. Chase tried to lift his legs so that he didn't step on any of the cars. Chase slowly retreated back to the bedroom. Chase was amazed how much of these robots were there. Clank! The front door of the bedroom opened. As David walked inside with a croissant still in his mouth.

"Hello?" asked David

"Yeah, David what are these things?" asked Chase

David entered the room. As more and more cars exited the bathroom. After a few seconds for David to react to what happened. David's expression clearly changed. David jumped and dived into the ground to stop the robots.

"Oh God. Do not let them out. Help me get them," shouted David

Chase, still in shock, closed the door behind. David got up and turned on his computer and used a program to shut down the car robots.

"Oh, what was that!?" asked Chase.

"That was my mini cleaning robot. That I programmed and started using about yesterday." answered David.

"I was trying to find you, but no one was here. And I heard some noises in the bathroom. I found these cleaning robots by accident." said Chase

David grabbed a sticky note and wrote it down. *"Performed well, but made noise"*.

"It's ok. You actually helped me improve these things." said David

"Well, bye. I Still need to eat breakfast." said Chase

Chase quickly egressed the room and walked toward the dining area. David grabbed one of the robots and started to add some parts or deleting some parts to fix the sound problem.

After fifteen minutes, Chase finished his breakfast and walked back to his room and started to check what had happened to their rocket that they sent about 5 months ago. The tracking states that the rocket has gone about eight quintillion miles far off to space. However there were some connection errors, for example when it was at exactly six million miles the system had an intermission and stopped moving for 6 hours and it started moving again.

The strange part is that when it stopped, the rocket froze in mid-space. It did not move a single bit. It seemed like something usurped the spaceship. The rocket was torpid compared to how it should have been. When the engine and the system started to work again, everything was brittle. About ten minutes later, everything became regular again. Chase was lackadaisical in this event at first. However, there were more cases of the rocket just malfunctioning and stopping in the middle of space.

Chase spent about two and a half hours watching the time lapse. Trying to find and gather the information and the events that were caught during the five months. There was something that caught Chases' eyes. At the two and a half month period, during noon; all the cameras blacked out. The only camera that was not blacked out was the outside one. It's job was supposed to show the body of the rocket. All of the cameras blacked out. A quarter of a second later, it started back up. Through the outside camera, a quick flash of light appeared and disappeared. Also at that second the rocket was not visible. The only thing that was visible was the stick that held the outside camera sticking out of the light.

Chase thought it was just a system issue, however the blacked out and the flash happened at the same moment. At first sight, the scene looked natural and quite smooth actually. Since Chase was watching a time lapse; the speed was incredibly quick, also disappearing and the appearance only took about a quarter of a second. Despite the quickness, Chase somehow managed to catch the event through the second watch. While Chase was still tangled in the webs of mysteries, a new religion was born.

Chaper:

"A group of Susitians; dressed in regular daily cloth, have surrounded the Central Universe Building, They seem possessed by something, walking in the same motion." said the reporter

"URG, AMM, ARGG" said the Susitians,

BANG, BANG, KLANK!

"Oh God, the Susitians have began smashing the..the..Central... ulging" shouted the reporter.

The T.V blacked out.

"Hm, I guess it worked." said a figure

"We will need more macrocosmbeings to actually make the "process work"." said another figure,

"I guess it is a good start,"

"No, different macrocosmbeings have different minds. The "process" has to be "improved"."

"We need to study and test at least one native macrocosmbeing from each and every planet." said another figure.

"There is a human that has some special power. We can use its power to take over."

"We don't need the human, we have a whole army of experienced Uldian soldiers,"

"Yes, but we can make clones of the human, and suck out the power of the human. That would make us stronger,"

"I'll research about this human being, maybe we will use it."

Meanwhile, Chase just sat in the room for two and a half hours, trying to figure and connect the mysteries together.

Knock, Knock.

"Hello" said Chase

"Yeah, it's me. Kate." answered Kate

"Okay, come on in," responded Chase

"What are you doing?" asked Kate

"Watching the time lapse of the rocket we sent five months ago." answered Chase

"Oh, can I join."

"Sure, let's go to the central area. And I'll call David."

"Okay"

Kate headed out the door. She quickly ran toward her room and grabbed her laptop. Chase grabbed his phone, and called David.

"*Dude, Central lab, now.*" said Chase

"*Okay! Do I need to bring anything?*" asked David

"*Yeah, your laptop*"

"*K, see you in 5 minutes.*"

Chase walked out of the door, seamlessly scrolling through his phone. He kept walking down the empty hallway. Suddenly, a scent of coldness thrived through his bones. Chase's vision was blackened. Chase fell, it seemed like Chase was falling into unknown blackness. It seemed like his soul was sucked out of his hollow corpse. Chase felt extreme pain. The emptiness Chase felt ignored the pain. Chase's mind suddenly was filled with fear, anger, and loneliness. With the last breath, Chase opened his eyes, and saw a tall and skinny dark creature beside him.

"When do you think Chase is going to come?" asked Kate

"I don't know, he should be here now," answered David

"Yeah, he said he was going to come right after he called you," added Kate.

### Five Minutes Passed

"He is still not here, we should try to find him," suggested David,

David stood up and calmly walked out of the central lab area. David walked toward Chase's bedroom, bathroom, living room, and the kitchen. Chase was nowhere to be found. David had a bad feeling. He thought something had happened to Chase. Kate searched the basketball court, the basement, and their parent's office. Nothing was found, no Chase, no traces of Chase.

*Tic, tic, tic.* As seconds and seconds passed by, nothing was found. Apprehensiveness began to fill Kate and David's mind. However, there was a large and weird foot mark on one of the hallways. It was the exact same hallway Chase stepped foot on. David and Kate at first just walked past it or just ignored the foot mark. After searching for Chase for thirty minutes. Kate and David had no choice but to call the parents and ask for help.

After a day of searching, the police were called, helicopters arrived, missing signs were put up. However, still no sign of Chase was found.

# CHAPTER 5

"Woah, where the heck am I?" said Chase. As he woke up full of cold sweat. Chase found himself in a mysterious place. The surrounding had a medieval theme, however more advanced technology. Chase realized he was "strapped" onto a seat with mysterious balls on top of them. At first, Chase was confused that he could not move. Virtually, nothing was attached to him that could have strapped him. As Chase struggled more trying to "unstrap", he realized a beam of reflective light cuffed his hand onto the seat and another beam of light was tightened across Chase's chest onto the seat.

"Oh, what the!" said Chase.

Before CHase realized, a tall skinny dark creature hitted him. And Chase passed out again.

"Where do you think Chase went?" asked David

"I don't know, but I think something took him. He didn't leave by himself." responded Kate.

"Yeah, hope we find him soon." added David.

As the parents have already lost some hope. It has been five days since CHase disappeared into nowhere. The whole house was depressed, having someone they love just disappear into the air; leaving no trace and no hope. The house seemed sad, dark, and hopeless. It seemed like hope had been squeezed out of their soul. The investigation went nowhere, and left the house heartbroken. However, the investigation was still happening. There was little hope, but it was still hope. Even so, the whole investigation has gone to nothing. Even so, it has been five long days and nights, and nothing was found. Even so, the family doesn't even know if Chase is even alive. There was still a little hope, and a little bit of trust.

Chase woke up again in sweat for the second time. The setting was different. It seemed like Chase was in a jail cell. There were light blue beams of light trapping Chase inside a large white room. The white room had nothing but a bed, a toilet, a sink, and a table. Chase did not know how to react. About ten minutes later, Chase felt no alone. He could sense macrocosmbeings around him. They were unnatural beings. It felt like they had special powers. It was not just one supernatural, he was surrounded by supernatural beings. He wondered if himself had special powers or something.

Chase thought there was no way he had special powers. He was just a regular human being, but somewhat smarter than others his age. But Chase did not feel out of place. He felt he was home.

Ziiii, Bang!

The wall between the cells has been dropped down, and the macrocosmbeings will be able to see each other now. As Chase was surprised and somewhat scared, he was able to see the other cellmates. Chase stood up and wandered around desperate to meet and greet the cellmates. While the wall dropped a figure randomly appeared right in front of the cells.

"HELLO. I may have your attention. Welcome to your new home. Do not get too emotionally and physically attached to each other. You beings will get put through extreme pain and death. We will remove your powers from you and use it against the world. It will be well appreciated if you support us and not make us go through difficulty while you die. The better you behave, the more comfortable you will die. Thank You. And may the process begin." said a white coated Uzabian.

"Who are you?" shouted a Nenalian crewmate.

The Uzabian did not answer the question. He just simply disappeared. As some of Chase's crewmates were confused. As some were angry. Chase was also baffled by what just happened. Chase did not hesitate to look around for help. However, he found nothing by confused faces.

Something caught Chase's eye while everyone was confused, a pretty Kingukian girl sitting on her bed. Chase blushed, as the girl noticed Chase and waved at him. Chase turned his head and blushed even more.

Suddenly, the girl appeared right in front of Chase. Chase nearly jumped up and had a heart attack.

"Holly cra.." said Chase.

"Hello. I saw you staring at me. So I came to say hi." said the girl.

"Can you please not do that again. My heart will jump out if you do that." responded Chase

"Sorry, let me introduce myself." said the girl.

"Okay.." said Chase

"My name is Kerlis Visk, I am from Kinguk. A beautiful planet. And my power is teleportation. As you can tell. And what is your power?" said Kerlis.

"Well, first of all, my name is Chase Hudgson. I am from Earth. Second of all, I have no idea what you are talking about. I don't think I have any power." responded Chase.

"That's impossible. They only capture macrocosm beings' with supernatural powers. That is why you are here, your powers will get "sucked" out." stated Kerlis.

"Maybe I don't know what my power is yet." said Chase

"Yeah, that is probably the case." said Chase

"Anyway, it was nice to meet you." said Kerlis.

"Yeah, sure," said Chase.

The girl disappeared and appeared back on her bed. Chase looked around and wanted to meet more crewmates. Chase also thought that he had some special power. Anyways, Chase stopped looking around, and just laid on his own bed. After the wall between the rooms was put back up. Chase quickly fell asleep, and was back to the white background. However, this time it was something different.

Chase saw a dim line of words flowing in the air. At the distance Chase was standing at, he could not see a single word. As Chase walked toward the line of words, a small oval appeared on top of the line of words. Inside, Chase could only see a glimpse of space. It seemed it was a portal leading him to somewhere. Once, Chase arrived at the words, and read the line of words. He was excited, surprised, and somewhat confused. The line of words stated.

*The h'ro hast the pow'r to abs'rb. The pow'r of charm speaking. The pow'r of telekinesis. The pow'r of Heal.*

"Wow, I have never realized any of this." said Chase, speaking to himself.

"How do I use it though?" Chase asked himself.

As soon as Chase said the line. He was sucked toward the portal-like circle.

"Ahh!" cried Chase

Chase tried to use telekinesis to hold on. But he did know the way, and was sucked into the portal.

Chase entered a similar room, there was a new line of words in the distance. CHase unreasonably walked toward the floating line. Halfway through, Chase realized the line was the same exact line.

"Hello, welcome to the power tutorial, please fill in the form!" said a random woman.

A white tablet dropped out of the sky, Chase picked the thing up. And was confused.

"*Please fill in the questions given below. 1. What are your main powers?* That would be these two, and those two. *2.What is a personality?* Outgoing, and sure brave. *3.What is your name?* Chase Hudgus." read Chase.

"Thank you. Be patient and your result and your trainer will be picked soon." said the voice.

The tablet disappeared, and Chase's mind was still lost in a fog of confusion.

"Okay?!"

About one and a half minutes later, a huge cylinder gracefully fell and landed on the white soft floor. A woman and a young Fadepikian male, walked toward Chase. Chase backed up naturally. But the Fadepikian stopped him.

"Hey, no need to be afraid. I am your power trainer." shouted the Fadepikian.

Chase stopped and walked toward the woman and the guy. Once they reached a communicable distance, the guy introduced himself and the power program.

"Hello, my name is Faderion. I am a professional trainer with telekinesis and charm speaking. I will be your trainer during your dreams." said the Fadepikian.

"So what are you going to teach me?" asked Chase

"Oh, yeah we never explained it to the boy. This is supernatural power training. So you have some supernatural powers and we will help you develop you to your full potential." explained Faderion.

"Okay, and who are you, ma'am?" asked Chase

"I am the batte robot and the leader of the SPAS" answered the lady.

"What exactly does SPAS mean?" asked Chase

"It means "Supernatural powers action school"" answered Faderion.

"Okay, so when do we start the training?" asked Chase again.

"Tomorrow night. Tonight is about to be over. So goodbye!" answered Faderion.

Everything disappeared, a massive hole appeared underneath Chase. Chase fell into complete darkness.

"Chase! Chase! Wake up!" shouted Kerlis.

Chase slowly opened his eyes. But the brightness was too much. He shutted his eyes right after the brightness got to him.

"What?" said Chase as he used his eyes to block the bright white light.

There was Kerlis. Sitting next to Chase, trying to wake him up.

"Get up, they are serving breakfast right now." answered Kerlis.

Chase shot right up the bed. Kerlis jumped up in surprise.

"Wow, that was fast!" said Kerlis.

"I am so hungry! I didn't eat yesterday." said Chase. Chase blurrily looked around and saw the cellmate already got and started eating.

Chase got up and walked toward the food cart that was placed in the middle of the room. Chase quickly walked to the cart. There were two choices for the Earth-like planet beings. There were eggs, bacon, and pancakes. The other choice was two sandwiches. As Chase tried to grab the first choice, he realized that he wouldn't be full just.

Without hesitating, Chase took both of the meals and walked back to his table. Chase sat on his chair, and started ravenously eating. Luckly, the meals were enough for him. Later during the day, Chase was introduced to Orla, a Trildian girl with a shy personality. Gordom is an Aesamapian boy, a strong and brave teenager. Lastly, Chase met a Rebelaskian female, her name was Rebela, and she was married to a man but she was divorced.

After meeting the cellmates, nothing was left to do. The rooms had nothing but a bed and a bathroom. Nothing was there for any of them to stay active. Quickly, everyone was stuck in the boredom atmosphere. Even though nothing was there to do, everyone was tired. They didn't talk to each other. Mayhem everyone was sad and confused, that once they had a happy life on their planet. One night later, everything was gone. People they love are gone, things they own are gone. Wondering if their supernatural powers are good or bad.

On one side, the powers make them special. And they can do things other beings are unable to do.

On the other hand, they are trying to take their powers away. Makine regular life very difficult and annoying to handle. They cannot hangout with regular people. People view them as friendly. Not a friend.

The first time, they felt left out. Not wanting the power anymore. It is interrupting what they could have had.

In one case, Gordom's specialty is indestructibility and super-healing. Even though his body is indestructible. His feelings are destructible, he has been living for six hundred years. He could not get a regular life.

Could not make friends.

Could not find love.

Could not find a stable life.

Could not do a single thing about it.

Without watching things come and go. Birth and death. Everything he meets, will die right in front of his eyes. He can do nothing, but watch. Supernatural powers, is it a good thing?

# CHAPTER 6

The next day, the same thing as yesterday. About a week passed, and the cell was dull. It seemed like everything was dead in there. Boredomness has filled their brain with anger and desperateness for help. During the afternoon, the white coat dude came to check on Chase and his cellmates again.

"Hello! I hope you all are doing well" shouted the white coat.

"Get us out of here!" shouted Gordom.

"Well, I was just able to say. Would I have a volunteer to go for a "walk" really quick. Since you wanted so much to get out. I assume you are a volunteer. **Soldiers** get him out!"

"**HA!** I am indestructible, you cannot possibly hurt me. Weak!" responded Gordom.

"Hem. We'll see!"

"Leave him alone." said Chase

"OH, another one. You will be the second one then." said the white coated.

As a heavily armed creature busted in a cell. And grabbed Gordom and left. The rest could not do a single thing.

Tik, Tac, Tik, Tac. Second after seconds, the sound of time filled their timeless minds. Second after seconds, Gordom has not returned. Second after seconds, there was nothing left to do, but waiting for their doom. It was like the tik, tac resembled the rain of desperation, powerless, and fear hitting onto their defenseless bodies with no hope. The emptiness filled their chest. The emptiness hurted the weak feelings and bodies. The more time passed, the more dark thoughts came to them.

DOOM! The cell was busted open, and Gordom was carelessly thrown onto the cell ground. They stared at him and hurried him onto the bed. Gordom was weak, pale. He seemed mental weakened. It seemed like something was sucked out of his poor core.

The white coated guy appeared again in front of the cell.

"What have you DONE to him?!" shouted Chase

"A little drink and massage with him." said the white coat.

"How DARE you!!" shouted Kerlis.

"Heal him. OR I WILL!!" shouted Rebela.

"Oh, your powers will not work in this center. Also the human boy is going next." responded the white coat with a sneer.

A skinny and black creature walked inside the cell. The creature was about nine feet tall, and its skin looked shiny. It had a large mouth with no eyes; and it had huge hands. The creature grabbed Chase one handed and took him out of the cell.

The other cellmates could not do anything. They felt fear and was paralyzed around the large creature. Everytime the monster was near, a cold and dark feeling came upon them. Their skin was tightening up. They would begin to release cold sweat.

The monster knocked Chase unconscious and was brought to a medical room. The main difference is, none of the equipment was supposed to heal. There were ray guns, claw hands, and many more harmful equipment. Before Chase could turn to the other side, a huge ball of an unknown metal was pointed in front of Chase. Chase couldn't say anything at the moment. About five seconds later, a beam of light was sucked out of Chase's chest. At first, Chase felt nothing but heat coming out. A few moments later, Chase began sweating like crazy. While the sweat was dripping, he felt extreme pain from his chest. It felt like his chest was going to be ripped apart into thousands of pieces.

"AHG!" agonized Chase.

The pain was so intense that Chase almost fainted. Chase tried to put out his hand and use telekinesis to push the machine away. However, it didn't work. About thirty seconds later, the white coated being came into the room and was ginning right at Chase.

"Well, well, well. Now who is the one in charge." sneered the white coat.

Chase could not respond. Chase stared at the white coat.

The white coat looked onto a tablet attached to the machine. A laugh. Came from the white coat.

"We can stop now. This boy is almost dead." said the white coat.

A female came into the room and stopped the machine. Chase was exhausted. Without another thought, Chase langed toward the white coat and tried to punch him. However, he was once again knocked out. Chase was thrown in the cell and woke up. He saw Kerlis getting grabbed by the creature.

BOOM! Chase shot right up, and was staring right at the creature. Even though the creature has no eyes, it's attention was caught. There was flame in Chase's eyes.

"Put her DOWN!" shouted Chase.

The creature ignores the demand.

Chase's muscles were burning. It felt like some kind of energy attached to Chase. Chase ran and jumped toward the creature and made a hard punch right in the chest. The creature fell, and so was Kerlis. Chase carried Kerlis in mid-air and landed on his feet. Kerlis was put on the side. As Chase's muscle burnt more, he started flowing in the air. There were red particles around Chase, and Chase's fists became pure red. He ran full speed toward the creature and punched the creature right in on the head.

"GAHHH!" shouted the creature.

Chase continued to punch the creature. At last, the creature fainted right in front of the cell. Chase threw the creature across the hallway. He re-entered the cell. And laid on his bed. Everyone was amazed. Rebela's eyes were wide open, and Kerlis was even more amazed. Kerlis's affection for Chase grew like a ton. Chase who was just laying there like nothing just happened.

About five minutes later, the staff member of the center came and was confused about what had happened. They are meeted with the fainted creature in the beginning of the hallway. As the security was called and weapons were pulled out. At first the staff was confused who could have possibly defeated this monster. Chase and the rest of the cell was questioned by a machine. Later the security camera caused every second of what happened.

Chase was put in solitary confinement for 3 days and was released back to the regular cells. One night, Chase was brought back to the white room again. This time Faderion was standing there waiting for Chase.

"Hey. Ready to learn how to utilize your powers?" asked Faderion.

"Yeah! I have a question though. I don't know what happened when my fist was red and I was floating." said Chase.

"Yeah, I am not sure what happened there, but I know that is not a regular power." responded Faderion.

"Okay? Anyways, I want to learn telekinesis. Is that okay? Or do we have to learn something else?" asked Chase.

"Yeah, we can learn telekinesis. That's fine!" answered Faderion.

"Yeah, so first you have to get your mindset right first. And sit down." continued Faderion.

Chase slowly sat down and closed his eyes.

"Yes, very good. Now think about a thousand bullets going at 500 miles per hour straight toward you." announced Faderion calmly.

In Chase's vision, he was in a dark room with thousands and thousands of bullets going straight at him.

Chase's veins became more intense. He was focused, his full intention was on stopping the bullets. Faderion pulled out a tablet from the skies. It showed a chart of some kind.

"Good! Now imaginarily put your hand up in front of the bullets." said Faderion.

The chart showed the amount of centration Chase had on stopping the bullets. Regular humans' concentration level is usually at forty-five percent, however due to the supernatural power, Chase's concentration level is usually at fifty-five percent. However, the concentration level needs to reach one hundred percent to stop something small and light. In order to be able to drive a car, the concentration needs to be at two hundred percent for at least thirty seconds.

Learning telekinesis is extremely easy, however the training is more than extreme. Chase's concentration has been going up quickly. A shake can be seen on some of the bullets. Even though Faderion could not see it, Chase's expression made it clear that he was improving. The highest level of concentration Chase was at was eighty-six percent. That is very impressive for someone to try for the first time.

Faderion called for Chase and stopped him.

"Hey Chase, you did a really good job," said Faderion.

"What? Not a single bullet stopped." said Chase.

"Yeah I know, but it was very impressive for someone to do that for the first time." responded Faderion.

"Sure."

"Yeah. Make sure to never over-work. It can damage your brain if you try too hard."

"Yeah, I felt kind of dizzy after you called me."

"Anyway, let me explain how telekinesis works"

"Okay"

After that Faderion explained the percentage of concentration and levels. Chase was excited to master telekinesis.

"OH!" said Chase. As he woke up, Chase just woke up and it seemed like they were moving. However, everything inside the room was still the same. The only thing different is that the view of the window was changed.

Chase didn't think any difference of this, not until they arrived at their destination. Before, they were in a four bed cell, with nobody else next to them. Now, Chase's cell arrived at a new prison. There were all kinds of people there. The prison was huge. Chase measured the prison was about 17 football fields from where he could see. There could be even more, the end could not be seen in Chase's vision. The prison is full of prisoners. It was about 50 stories tall, and each room had two prisoners in each of them.

Chase was sent into a room on the 4th floor. The guards said that there were levels of danger. The first is the weakest and all the way to the 17th is the most dangerous to contain.

About fifteen minutes later, another being was brought inside the cell. It wasn't Kerlis, Rebela, nor Gordom. An inventor like a human was put inside with Chase.

"Ello, mate" said the human suddenly.

"Oh, hello." responded Chase.

"What ya power?" asked the old man.

"Um, telekinesis, charmspeaking, absorbing, and another power that I don't know." answered Chase.

"Nice mate, me power is being smart? And looking young." joked the human.

"I am sorry, I should have introduced myself first." continued the human.

"Me name is Erik, Erik Beasly. Folks around here call me the inventor. Also I am from England on Earth." said Erik.

"Good to meet you Erik, I am Chase Hudgus and I am also a human," responded Chase.

"Well, I'll get some rest. Goodtime." said Erik as he closed the wall between the beds.

"Oh well. I guess I will rest too!" said Chase to himself.

Chase laid on his bed and faded into deep sleep.

# CHAPTER 7

Chase has been lost for 2 months now. No sign of him was seen, nor heard. The family has quieted the search for Chase. Everyone has gotten back to their regular life, however they still believed Chase was still somewhere in the universe. In Kate and David's minds Chase was somewhere far away into the galaxy. Far far away from home Earth. The mission to get Chase back would not be easy but it is still possible. For the past four weeks, they have been trying to locate where Chase is using the rocket they have sent. They have been making progress, but to the speed they are working at, it would take hundreds of years until Chase would be found. David has tried to contact system-class scientists and detectives to help them but, the result they would get is no.

One of the good things they discovered is a new type of energy. Nothing they had seen before, the mineral is powerful and rare. However, during the journey to find Chase. The rocket discovered a large planet full of this mineral. David had started to construct another model of the original rocket but has a massive amount of storage.

This might be the energy to defeat the virus.

However, there was one person they haven't contacted. That is the one and only Tony Musk. At first, David thought they stole from him. And secondly, he thought the technology wouldn't be advanced enough. But that was the only choice they had left.

*Dear Mr. Musk,*

*We ask you for your help. My friend Chase has been lost far away in the universe. We need your help to bring Chase back. You might be thinking, why would I help these kids. However, we have discovered a large amount of unknown minerals. It is rare and powerful. We would like to talk to you in person and bring a sample of the mineral.*

*Please for the love of the world.*

*Sincerely,*

*Chase's Friend David.*

The email was sent, hope of fire lighted once again. The sound of time dripped near David's Ears. Tik, Tac, Tik, Tac, David uneasily spined his chair around and waited for a response. A light hologram of David's dead brother stood in the corner, it looked right at David.

"Hey, long time no see." said the hologram.

"Max, is that you?" asked David.

""Yes, it is me. Hey, never give up, there will always be hope some-where." said Max

"What are you talking about, my best friend disappeared out of nowhere and we don't even have a sign of where he is." said David

"I have been watching, your friend is alive, somewhere in the universe. That is all I can tell you."

"I know!"

David shook his head and noticed the hologram disappeared. It seemed like he was dreaming. However, the hologram of his dead brother seemed so real. Finally, the tiredness had got to him. He hopelessly walked back to his room, and carelessly dived into his pain bed. Closed his dull and soulless eyes and rested.

Another day passed, David is still soullessly waiting for a response. Nothing could be done to stop waves of painfulness and coldness that keep hitting the families.

DING!

A notification popped on David's desktop.

David looked out and was surprised.

It was an email.

*Dear David,*

*My investments and my company haven't been doing that well. Through all the things the world is going through, I don't know if I am able to help you. But, life is all about trying. So if you want to show me the energy you were talking about. Come to my company building tomorrow at 12 a.m. And by yourself.*

*Sincerely,*

*Big T*

The light of excitement shone through David's eyes. It seemed like nothing could stop them. Finally, after failing, after failing, someone finally agreed to help them. As soon, the message was read, David rushed to pack the energy ready for Tony. However, there was a problem. How would he reach the building without his parents noticing? For the rest of the day, he had to design a plan. He had to get to the destination at 12 a.m, and come back to the house before 7 a.m.

Time is tight and concerning, arriving there would take 3 hours driving. Arriving and departing would take 6 hours. They have exactly one hour to discuss. After about 40 minutes, David came up with a transportation method.

Driving to the company building would take up too much time. Also the house would hear if someone went out if they drove. After minutes of consideration, David decided to use his old project. The 5p33d. A pair of shoes. Not just any ordinary shoes. It was fast. The shoes could make one run as fast as 430 mph. However, the friction of the speed would burn without protection.

So for the rest of the day, David was creating a suit. A fire protection suit, one that is light, protective, and dim to the background. The materials were enough, but time wasn't. David was racing with time. Every second, David had to focus.

5:00, 6:00,7:00, 8:00. Time is up. David had to leave. Even if he didn't finish. The suit was only sixty percent done. David continued working for 10 more minutes. Now, he had to leave. The pressure was on. David but the mostly finished suit inside a small bag. And stuffed the contained mineral inside. David also put on a vantablack jacket. He was set, David silently and swiftly jogged across the empty hallway.

Fortunately, no one was at the front entrance. However, at some point the parents would find him missing. David had to use an exercise to dodge the parents. He rushed back to his room and grabbed his phone. 1, 2, 3,4 ,5. Time was running. David would be late if he didn't go now.

David rushed back to the entrance and busted out of the building. He quickly ran to the side, and waited if the guardians would notice him. Pound, pound, pound, his heart was pounding and so was the tight time. No one came to check the entrance. David quickly put on the suit and was on the roads.

A while later, David slowed down to take a rest. At this point David Was about forty-five percent there. He pulled out his phone, and called Kate.

Back at the house....

Durr, durrr, durrrrrrr.

Kate picked up the phone.

*"Hello?"* answered Kate

"*Hello, I am out right now. Could you make an excuse for me.*" said David.

"*What? Where?*" responded Kate confusingly.

"*Yeah, not much time to explain. Just say that I have to go urgently because I had to meet up with some friends*" said David.

"*Okay, but you better explain what happened,*" said Kate.

David quickly stuffed the phone inside the backpack and started running again. The coldness warped its hands around David. This was expected to happen. David's bone became stiff and hollow. He had to keep running, no matter what happened. This somewhat helped, David could run faster due to the coolness. Due to the coldness in the dark night, the chance of producing heat.

Skrrrrrrrrrrrrrrrrrrrrrrrrrrrrrrrrrrt. Bam! A blaze of light suddenly flashed under David. The spark of fire increased more and more as David drifted across the empty road. The heat quickly overcame David. The velocity of David made the drift seem like forever. After David stopped, he quickly swung his leg and was trying to put out the small fire. After the fire was finally put out, David had to find a solution to the fire not constantly blazing on David. David figured his coldness in the air is canceling the fire on his upper body. However, his feet are making the most contact between the ground. The best way to avoid direct contact and more friction with the ground is by rolling instead of running. However, he did not have wheels to put under his feet. The thought of it was in mind, but he had no material to quickly make a scooter.

David had to keep running, time was tight and opportunity was a pity. The good thing was, deeper into the night, the air was cooler. Flames did not appear as often, and the heat friction created kept David somewhat lukewarm. The rest of the voyage there was pretty smooth.

Blackness surrounds David as the freezing cold air whispers to David. As David got closer and closer to the empty black building, trees overcame the visible area. The lines of leafs seemed to be laughing at David while the wind firmly blew the rocking leafs. As David looked around the surroundings, a figure was seen near the massive building. David assumed the figure was the great Tony Musk. As David got closer and closer to the figure. Something was wrong about the figure. Something is very wrong. Extremely Wrong.

# CHAPTER 8

The figure's body shape became a weird dome shape. It somehow had antlers, and the closer David gets the body gets larger and larger. The point where it made no sense and no possibility that the creature was Mr. Musk. David froze in the air to figure out what possibly the strange creature could be. Suddenly the large creature started slowly walking toward David. As the creature came closer and closer, David felt a state of fear overcoming the air. David started backing up. The creature came closer.

Bam, bam, bam. The creature started running toward David. As human nature, David backed up and was somewhat scared. As the creature got closer and closer. A bright light started to shine through David's backpack. As the creature started sprinting at David. The closer the creature got the brighter the light shined. As sweat overflows David's scared body.

Somehow the creature started backing up. David was confused and scared. He started walking up to the building. The creature started getting far away from David. As David gets closer and closer. The creature began walking toward David again. Somehow the light shined brighter than it ever did. David in concern opened up his backpack to see what was going on. As soon as the backpack was open, the creature screamed.

"GAHHHHHHHHH" shouted the creature.

David quickly jumped on his feet in surprise. Held the glowing stone in his cold hand. The creature's skin changed dramatically. There was steam shooting out of the creature's horns. It seemed mad and angry. The creature started running fastly toward David at surprise. As soon as David realized the creature was 15 feet away from him. David held up the glowing stone as a self defense. As soon as the creature made contact with the stone. Instantly, the stone blasted a beam straight through the creature's body. David, in fear, quickly dropped the stone and ran inside the building. After a few seconds, David realized how powerful the stone they discovered in outer space was. And quickly ran outside the building and gathered his bag and the stone. After entering the main lobby, David turned to the right where a humanoid creature was standing. And there was. The Great Tony Musk.

David quickly jogged to the great figure and greeted the great. As soon as David approached him. A warm feeling overcame the cold air, a feeling of hope and excitement burned through David's cold body.

"You must be the great David. It nice to finally meet you." said Tony Musk

"No! Pleasure to meet YOU. Finally seeing the great Big T in person." responded David.

"Well, let's get started. Please come with me." said Tony Musk as he pointed toward an elevator.

David quickly ran toward the elevator and opened the door for Tony. As he pointed inside the elevator.

"Oh no, we don't use that here," said Tony Musk.

"Oh! Well, I should have known, because the high-tech in this building." said David awkwardly.

"Anyways, please enter the cell lifter and press the top button when you are in." said Elon Musk.

As David entered an ellipse shaped cell where a bunch of buttons were placed on the side of the cell. David remembered he had to press the top button in order to get to Tony's office. As David looked at the top of the side and saw a large red button. As David negligently pushed the button. David made an asinine and imbecile mistake. He did not realize the speed and the acceleration of the elevator.

ZOOM. The elevator shot right upped the tunnel. At first David's response system did not sense the high speed that they were leaving the ground. Then when the system detected the speed, it scared the living soul out of David. As David in natural response put both of hands on each side of the glass and waited. As the elevator shot right up the stealthy building, a gleam of bright redness shone across David's cold skin. David slowly turned toward the gleam of light. What greeted him was a sight of a gratifying and bewitching crack of dawn of the glorious Earth. Hope and aspiration was once gone, however now the torch of life was lit brighter and ever.

**DING DONG. Welcome to the Wonderful floor of Big T.** There David was at last the office of Tony Musk. As David furiously looked around the room. A figure was standing there confused.

"Hey, David. What took you so long to get to the Floor of Big T?" asked Tony Musk.

"Um, I was curious ...about the ....elevator and the ...view. Yeah" said David awkwardly.

"Well, anyway. Please enter the office." said Tony Musk.

As David entered the darkened room, Tony Musk disappeared.

"Hello?" said David confusingly

No response.

"Hello, Mr.Musk. Are you here." shouted David.

No response.

David became more anxious and started furiously walking around trying to find Tony Musk.

As time passed, no sign of Tony Musk was heard nor seen. It once was a calm walk, then it became a heavy run.

Heh, heh, heh.

"Mr. Musk?! Where are you? Hello?" shouted David.

As David finally stumbled across an area he has never been to. The area had a weird entrance, the door was an upside down door, with the door knob being a water bottle. David awkwardly slid through the door. And came upon the unexpected.

An army of hanged upside down clones of Tony Musk was there in the room. As David came upon the unusual scene, the entrance door behind him shutted dead.

As David turned arounded back to the clones, their eyes opened up. Staring into David's poor soul.

"Whahahahahahah. Mwahahaha" shouted the clones suddenly.

David looked up in fear. The robotic clones' eyes started glaring out bleams of blood red light. Suddenly, the background started to swivel. Then the tables began moving. David started to get dizzy. Everything started shaking, however the clones did not even move a single bit. As the room continued to shake, he realized something weird. David stood still and tried to relax and calm down. However, what he heard he could never forget.

# CHAPTER 9

Biiii,Buuuuuuu,Biiiii,Buuuuu. This continued for 10 minutes. "Ahhh" shouted Chase.

Chase finally woke up from his deep sleep. Chase tried to lift his body out from his bed but he could not. He seemed heavy, it seemed like everything was heavy. Doing anything was hard for him. Chase's memory was vivid, however something that was clear was he was locked up. As Chase finally was able to sit up, he instantly started looking around. There was a metal table near the concert wall, a toilet on the other side and a line of bars. As soon as Chase knew it, he was thrown out of the cell onto the lobby area on floor 4th. Chase looked back confused. He didn't see anything behind him the whole time.

Suddenly, a familiar face appeared about 50 feets away from Chase. An old man with pure white hair and a big big smile waved at Chase.

"G'mornin mate, yu finally fynale decided to wakeuup innit mate." shouted Erik.

"Hello Erik, how long have I been sleeping again?" asked Chase.

"Mate, you been sleepin fo 2 days." responded Erik.

"No wonder it was so hard to wake up. I had no energy"

"Oh yeah mate, there som wofuls and baykuhns over there."

"Ok, thanks."

Chase quickly egress from Erik, and walked toward the consuming area. Chase realized something, at floor 4 there are actually more humanoid creatures than other creatures. Chase kept on walking toward the area and accidentally bumped into a familiar figure.

"Ahh, ouch," said the familiar figure.

"Oh, I am so sorry." said Chase as he looked up in surprise.

"Chase?!" asked the figure.

"Kerlis, is that you?" asked Chase.

"Oh, my god it is you." answered Kerlis.

"Hello, how have you been?" asked Chase

"Well, I have been fine until they threw me in a jail cell."

"Yeah, me too. I met this old dude who seems pretty cool."

"Oh, what happened here?"

Kerlis gently placed her soft hand on the cheek of Chase.

"What?"

"There is a small scare here."

Without Chase noticing, he blushed insanely. His face became as red as cherries. However, Kerlis realized the insane blushing.

"Um... Are you ok?" asked Kerlis

"Yeah I am fine, why?" responded Chase

"Your face turned super red"

"Oh what."

Chase's face became more red than ever. Chase felt extreme heat explode across his red face.

"Um, it's nothing. Anyways, I am fine, thank you, bye.." said Chase

Suddenly Chase turned around and quickly egressed from the awkward situation.

"Wait...." whispered Kerlis

Chase quickly disappeared from the crowd and headed toward the cafeteria. Chase quickly grabbed breakfast and finished the simple meal. After grabbing breakfast, Chase wandered around the entire 4th floor. Nothing much was there, except for an uncountable amount of creatures that were locked up in the prison. Later in the afternoon, the 4th floor prisoners were brought out to the courtyard. Different prisoners were brought to different sections because the need to survive is different.

Chase was sent to an Earth-like courtyard, where Erik was also sent there. Chase walked around the massive land. Chase estimated that the land was about one acre. There were huge glass barriers surrounding the land. At first glance the courtyard was huge, Chase naturally walked around the massive yard. To his surprise there were actually lots of humans. Chase walked to the glass barriers out of curiosity. Chase carefully reached out to interact with the border. However, a strange force stopped him from doing that. Chase used a little bit more force toward the barrier.

ZOOM! Chase was suddenly ejected flying across the courtyard and landing harshly on the other side of the courtyard.

"Ouch, I should not have done that." Chase said to himself.

"Oh my god, are you ok?" asked a random humanoid creature.

"Yeah, I am fine. Sure." answered Chase

Chase carelessly made an attempt to stand up but failed ruthlessly. Again Chase made another attempt to stand up, out of nowhere a familiar figure appeared and assisted Chase on to his feet.

"Thank you..." said Chase

"Welcome." answered the figure

"Oh, wait. You look familiar. Your name was Jordan... Gordon..." said Chase

"Gordom." suggested Gordom

"Yes, yes. Gordom. Right"

"Anyways, be careful next time. No mindlessly interacting with things in the prison." advised Gordom.

Chase walked around while scratching his head. About 40 minutes later, Chase and the rest of the prisoners were brought back into the building. After sanitation, Chase headed back to his cell and rested on his plain bed. And faded into deep sleep.

Chase was back at a familiar place. There is plain white everywhere. Where the border could not be seen.

"Hello there, long time no see." said a figure.

"Oh, long time no see. Faderion." responded Chase.

"Oh, cool you remembered my name." said Faderion

"Anyways, I have a question."

"What's your question?"

"Why did I not get into this dimension thing for so long."

"I might not explain this to you, but we won't see each other often. The first reason is that there are millions of super beings who are waiting to be trained. Coaches are limited and sometimes supernatural abilities are difficult to train and practice. Second reason is that telekinesis is one of those abilities that is easy to teach but hard to master. You don't really need a coach twenty four seven watching you to assist you. So I hope that explains it to you."

"Okay..Yeah that somewhat explained the situation."

"Ok, now let's get into the training. Today we are doing physical drills to get you stamina, focus time, and strength up."

"Wait, how I am supposed to practice telekinesis, I can't use my powers inside the prison."

"Oh, good question. A period of time will bring you to a power training area. Where you can practice telekinesis. I am not sure why but, they say they want your powers to be the absolute best when they suck it out."

"Wait, have you been there before?"

"Um, unfortunately yes, I was an escapee with 5 different prisoners. That is why I live in this dimension now. They can't find me."

"Um, I don't know how to respond to that, but should we just continue with the training?"

"Yeah we should. Before the sun rises."

Chase was teleported to another location where futuristic fitness equipment was located. Soon later Faderion appeared bringing with him a rubik's cube, some like a puzzle board, and a book-like object.

"Ok. Now we are going to start with a bit of running."

Chase nodded.

"Please follow me."

Faderion leads Chase to an eerie looking treadmill. It was quite big and Chase had never seen a treadmill looking more distinctive than this. For some reason, the inside of the machine was full of water. Chase looked around the impenetrable apparatus and turned around to ask questions that every neophyte would ask.

"Um, what exactly is this thing." asked Chase

"It's a speed training treadmill. It has quicksand in it to slow you down" answered Faderion.

"Gentleman, I wash my hands off this weirdness." joked Chase.

"Haha, that's funny." responded Faderion.

"Anyhow, you wanna hop on this thing." continued Faderion

"But how am I going to get out though?"

"You are going to wear a protection suit. And a machine will pull you out."

"Well, ok then."

Chase awkwardly jerked around with the machine. The machine had a bizarre amount of switches required to press while the baffled Chase moved aside and asked for assistents from a professional, leading to making him look like a goon.

Chase abandons the thought of ever interacting with equipment in this particular dimension. Chase moved along from the past incident, as Faderion called Chase to put on a moronic suit rather than a protection suit.

This particular time, Chase succeeded to do something without needing help, which is putting on a protection suit.

*Clap, Clap.* Suddenly, an enormous robot arm appeared out of nowhere. As dumbfounded as Chase already was, Chase stood there thoughtlessly staring into space. Without patients, the robot arm roughlessly got behind Chase and lifted Chase up without warning.

"Ahh, what the..." screamed Chase

Without permission the robot carelessly slammed Chase into the machine and started the machine.

"Woah, woah. Chill buddy. He is clearly not ready yet." interrupted Faderion.

*"Too slow. Waste my time."* responded the robot.

The two were arguing non stop, leaving the poor Chase struggling to stand up and activate the machine.

"AHHH MMM" shouted Chase

Faderion and the robot could tell it was an attempt to scream, but he couldn't. His face was half buried under quicksand.

"Oh shoot!" shouted Faderion

Faderion quickly progressed toward the machine. Quickly, Faderion used telekinesis and yanked Chase out of the quicksand.

"Oh my god, what was that?" cried Chase

"Um, we had some technical issues... Yeah.." responded Faderion

"No, I saw and heard you arguing over there. With the dumb robo...." shouted Chase

Chase pointed toward the direction, but could not spot the robot.

"See, nothing was nothing there. Told you."

"Yeah sure. Whatever. I almost died from that."

"Well, you didn't... sooo... bye."

"Wha......"

There Chase was. Again. Laying on his snow white bed. Staring into the flooded plainness of the vast ceiling. Each pixel of the ceiling is like a natural piece of art. Pixel?!... What Pixels....

"Woah... What is that? What..." whispered to himself. As Chase tried to focus more onto the ceiling, an out of place blackness appeared on top. The blackness is glitching in and out, it seemed like a real life glitch. Chase stood up, and walked around to try and observe the glitch. Out of curiosity, Chase touched it. Nothing...nothing.... The blackness did not have any texture and a physical feel to it. However, he could not feel the wall and his arm did not go through from the opposite of the glitch. Also there was a dramatic temperature change when through the blackness.

"What the... This seems like it can take you to somewhere else." said to himself

Endless possibilities are running and flooding Chase's mind. Chase figured to himself.

*I guess the only way to find out is to enter it. But first I should do some scouting first.*

Chase carefully stuck his inside the glitch and started to look around. The place was weird, there were colorful pipes on the ground and connected to the ceiling. There were also huge black walls with LED lighting that seemed like a part of a pc, but Chase quickly threw away the thought of that.

BEEP, BEEP, ZEE, ZOOM. An unusual robot roamed around the huge wall and started spraying the massive green wall. The robot was large, it seemed it had an eye in the middle of a kite shaped head. The strange machine was levitating in mid-air. It had a kite head and a kite shaped body. The two parts were connected by a vague beam of red light. The machine was somewhat fearsome looking. It was just roaming around, it seemed like it was powerful and dangerous.

Verrr, bibi. Suddenly, the robot turned toward Chase. Discovering someone was there. It shot a bright beam of light straight at Chase's face. Suddenly the robot quickly ascended toward Chase. Chase fearfully exited his head out of the hole. However, on second thought, I revisited the glitch. He meticulously peeped into the glitch... Nothing was there. The robot was gone, no sign of the robot could be seen. Chase scouted around the clearance, and finally decided to take a step in there. The process of getting into the glitch was somewhat difficult and inconvenient. The glitch was really small. The hole was only able to fit Chase's head. The solution was to rip hole of the glitch larger. Chase gripped onto the sides of the hole. Use as much force he could have used and started ripped apart from another. He made an endeavor to open the glitch and surprisingly it was working, but slowly.

As Chase got the hole to be able to barely fit his body, he floundered even more to open out a comfortable space to fit through. Eventually, he succeeded. However, the prison guards came, the haphazard timing made Chase baffled.

# CHAPTER 10

"*Sfh sfh, the end is near.*" the crowd of clones quietly sang.
"*Nothing can be done.*"

"Waiting for the end"

"*Until we are all let free*"

David stood there unconscious and confused. As the clones said, nothing could be done. David was desperate to move, however he just could not get it done. It seemed like he was locked onto an invisible wall. As David struggled more to get out of the helpless situation.

David kicked his foot and tried to move his torso, but he failed. As time moved on quickly, David accidentally kicked a spot on the wall.

Clank! Bong! Clang! Chee! The sound of machinery emerged from the background. The sound of machinery became louder and louder. A large hole unfolds from the gossy ground. As David fiercely turned his head tried to look deeper into the hole. But he was out of time.

Verrt. Verirrt. As each of David's hand cuffs was dislocated and unlocked. David's body started falling into the hole.

As David started to free fall, he started to look for ways to hang onto the side of the hole. However, he simply could not. Both sides of the wall are pasted with some kind of oil. David could not see what was on the bottom. The bottom was plain black. Nothing was visible. As David continued to free fall. Apprehensive thoughts sooner or later entered David's fearful mind. What could be down there may kill David. Or it might be helpful. As time passed by, David was still falling. An end could not be seen. However, a vivid glance of light shone across David's freezing body. The temperature in the tunnel is unviable low. David had no sense of time whatsoever in the tunnel. Deeper David fell into the tunnel, the brighter the light became. And faster David fell.

David made another attempt to see the bottom of the tunnel. And this time he saw something.

A pure white wall at the end of the mysterious tunnel.

"Oh no! I am done." David thought to himself.

David tried to hang on to the sides, however, the sides seemed to be widened. David thought it was the end for him. So he put his two arms around him and closed his eyes.

Vummmmmmm! A bright shine of white light blasted toward David.

"Ah! Where am I? Is this heaven? Am I dead." said David.

As David looked around unconscious and started to question himself.

"Is this a dream?" David whispered to himself.

"No this is not a dream. In fact you have entered another dimension." a voice echoed through the entirety of the room, which seemed not to have an end.

"Um, who am I talking to?" asked David.

"Oh, yes. How rude of me. My given name is Thomas. You can call me Tommy. I am the manager for the Tony Musk Inner Dimension." responded Tommy.

"Hello, anyways what is the Tony Musk Inner Dimension? And how did I not die from that fall?" asked David.

"Ah, yes. You did not die because you reached a certain speed where you are teleported to this dimension. And this dimension is a place where Mr. Musk can greet his guests in his true form." responded Tommy

"What do you mean "True Form"?" asked David

"You will find out yourself. Move along. Enough talking" said Tommy.

As a bubble of force lifted David up onto thin-air. David looked around the area, confused. David was still recovering from what happened and what was going to happen.

As the higher David was lifted, the more he hallucinated from what had happened. He started second guessing himself of this being fake. And considering that he could be dead, and this is just an afterlife dream. Suddenly, a change of color in the air occurred. As before the air was light and clear. However, it changed now to a tangerine colored atmosphere. As the temperature had a dramatic and climatic rise. The overall mood in that area changed intensely. About 2 minutes later, the lifting bubble reached its destination. The bubble arrived at a floating island where it was so high up, the bottom could not be seen. As a pocket was opened up for David to egress from the air bubble, a robot came out of a wall and greeted their confused and apprehensive guest.

David stepped out of the lifter and was greeted with a flying robot.

*"Hello, welcome to the upper floor of the great Tony Musks Inner Dimension!"* said the robot.

"Um, hello?!" said David

*"Yes, please follow me. Mr. Musk wants to speak with you."* said the robot.

The robot walked towards an abnormal door. The door had a green and blue stripe spiraling in a circle. As a pad of numbers emerged from the bottom, David's mind was wandering into nowhere. The spiral door opened. The blue and green stripes spun and opened up a passage for David to go in.

David entered the door. What awaits him was not ever expected.

At the end of the dark hallway, a glare stroke of light shot through David's pupil. David awkwardly walked toward the light source with his arm up in his face. The robot, located slightly right and in front of David. Increased its speed.

*"Speed up, we are already late. Mr. Musk needs to see you urgently."* said the robot.

Without a response, David started hogging toward the light source. Surprisingly, the tunnel was longer than how David thought it was. It seemed short, however it turned out the tunnel was about 50 yards.

Eventually, David reached the end of the tunnel. What met him made him dead silent.

Orange lights glaring out of a deformed body, a bulging head and lots of white facial hair on the skin. Multiple transparent unknown metal tubes were sticking out of the illogical body into one giant machine on each side of the body.

Suddenly, a glare of bright yellow light. Appeared above the unrecognized body.

"Hello!" said a young voice.

"Hello?! Who am I speaking to exactly?" said David baffled.

"Yes. It's me. Tony Musk the Great." said Tony Musk.

"Where are you exactly Mr. Musk?" asked David eagerly.

"Oh! I am the half-dead, half not dead corpse on the floor." responded Tony Musk.

"Um...." staddered David

"Yeah, it might be hard to accept me and my new form." said Tony Musk

"Ok?!" said David

"Anyways, tonight it is not about me. It is about me helping you."

David noticed, everytime Tony Musk spoke. The beam of light seemed to change in shapes. The outline of the light would move. At first, he thought nothing of this.

"Um..." responded David

"Anyways, do you have a certain crystal or material you found in space you want to show me," said Tony Musk.

"Oh, yes... Um... I might have not brought my backpack through the portal to this place."

"Ahh. I figured. Helllloooooo. CAN WE GET DAVID'S BAG IN HERE PLEASEEEE!" shouted Tony Musk.

A robot carelessly flew inside the room from the wall. And gently dropped David's torn backpack near Tony Musk's half-dead body.

"Um... Do you need me to open it." asked David

"No. You just sit there. Oh yeah. CAN WE GET A SPARE CHAIR IN HERE!!"

A circular robot shot right inside the room with a spare chair on top of it. It suddenly stopped making the chair fly across and landed where David was standing.

"Thank you...." said David

"No need to thank these robots. They are simply lifeless."

"....."

"Anyways, yes let me check this thing out."

"How..?" whispered David

"Don't ask questions. Just wait."

The line of energy stuck out of the light source and unzipped the backpack. And continued to take out the glowing purple stone.

The line of energy continued to look through the backpack.

"Is this all you have?" asked Tony Musk

"Um. No, we have more coming in. And a few more pounds at my house."

"Ok. Yeah. That's what I thought. Anyways, let's get to my lab."

The source of light above the body. Moved around and ordered David to deliver him to his lab.

A square hole on the ground, large enough for David to fit in. The hole was right below David. Causing David to fall again. This time, the hole is somewhat shallow. At the bottom, a squishy material was placed below to prevent fall damage. David hit the squishy material and saw a sign. "Sit In The Box. And Grab on Tight." As the sign said, a rail cart appeared in front of David.

David carefully sat on the railcar, grabbed onto the sides of the railcar.

A button slid down from the ceiling. "Please press this button when you are ready to survive mental pain."

As David pressed the button with no concern. Not yet..

# CHAPTER 11

"Where did you think you were going?" said the warden.

"I don't know. It was just there that morning." said Chase

"Do you think I am going to trust you?" said the warden.

"I am not going to hide anything. I really just found the hole there." said Chase

"Then how do you explain the action of you trying to get in the hole." responded the warden.

"Well. I was curious about what was in there."

"Alright we will further look into this. Just don't get yourself in trouble again. "

Chase cautiously walked out of the warden's office. Back to the central/dining area, where he unfortunately missed breakfast. Chase quickly walked past the dining area. And he heard a familiar voice.

"Hey Chase!" shouted Kerlis.

Chase hastily turned around to greet this familiar figure.

"Um. Hey. Whatssup." said Chase

"Yes. I heard you got in a bit of trouble here. And I am not gonna ask you about it. Because I know you had enough of this. So I just wanted to tell you I left you some food in your cell. I noticed you missed the breakfast period." said Kerlis

"Oh. Thank you so much. I was really hungry. Yeah. Ima go finish up my food and meet you later. Bye" said Chase

Chase quickly descended from the area and went back to his cell. However, he noticed, there was a group of enforcers there to investigate the portal. Due current state, Chase was moved to another cell.

Surprisingly, the food Kerlis left was still there. Chase sat on the chair and started to devour the food. Even though the food was quite cold, it was still good. As one says, everything is delicious if you are hungry.

Later, Chase finished his food and walked around the prison. This time, he was allowed to go down to floor 1, 2, and 3. As the creatures in those floors are weaker than Chase. Who is on floor 4. Obliviously, Chase was not allowed to hurt the creatures there. The rule does not apply to every level of the prison. This rule only applies to the first 5 levels in the prison. Chase proceeded to get down to level three.

The prisoners there were like humanoid creatures. But their physicality was not nearly as strong as regular humans. However, their head was exceptionally large. Nothing special was on floor three, so Chase decided to move along. Chase dropped down to floor 2 and what was there surprised him.

Large multicolored balls of slime roamed around floor 2. The weird creatures did not seem to have a physical body. It had a lighter colored outer body, and it seemed it stored some liquid inside of its slimy body. Walking around level two was more than difficult. The floor was covered with trail juice of the slimy creatures. Also, Chase had to be extra careful of stepping onto the slime creatures. Some were huge but somewhere microscopic. Another big issue of traveling at that level is the difficulty of visuals. Some of the slimes were dark colored, which made them easier to see. However, some were lighter. That made them impossible to notice. The cell was structured differently. The cell was overall smaller. The features inside of the cell changed as well. It had a sphere shaped bed. With two tubes sticking out of the wall. Chase thought it was some kind of cleaning feature, like a shower. Anyhow, Chase later descended to the first floor.

Chase walked to the entrance of the first floor and was surprised. He could not properly enter the floor. The door to the floor was impossible for humanoids to enter. Maybe some kind of humanoid in these universes can. But not Chase. The entrance of the borderline is unenterable. The size of the entrance was so small that Chase's hand. And Chase's hand is just a normal 16 year old male hand.

Defeated, Chase walked back to floor 4. Chase progressed toward his cell and proceeded to rest on this relentless bed. The warm and safe net that would catch him when everything goes against his will. The safe haven that people don't appreciate enough for. The thing that everyone could rely As Chase quietly fades into deep dreams. Somewhere in the vast universe something universal was born.

"THE GLORIOUS CHILD IS BORN. WE SHALL CELEBRATE THE FOR THE BIRTH OF THE NEW RULER!!!!" shouted a creature.

"YES. MY SON SHALL BE THE FUTURE RULER OF THIS UNIVERSE." shouted another creature.

"YEAH. YES... WHAT A LEGEND!" shouted the crowd

As the crowd continued to celebrate the birth of something great, an evil force was planning something. Something great, but immoral and purely evil.

"Yes.. The plan shall work. This will be the greatest and the most destructive plan in the history of the universe. MWAHAHAHAHAHAHA!" said the creature....

## *Later*

"Ahh. What was that? Oh that was just a dream." said Chase to himself

"But it felt so real," he said to himself again.

"Anyways, I should move on with my day..." he said

"Oh... What a surprise. It's night..."

"Of course, I slept during the day."

"What am I supposed to do now? I am too excited to sleep again."

"I can't do anything. My cell is locked up. And... Actually, I might be able to get this cell open."

Even though the cell is made out of Xuflium. Which is one of the toughest and the most expensive metals there is.

Chase jerked with the metal pole, but ultimately failed to do anything with the poll. Chase came up with an idea. An idea which could go both ways. Chase tried to use telekinesis to do something to get the cell open but nothing happened. As nothing was able to open the cell. If something had the ability to open the cell, Chase did not have enough skill and concentration skills to even lift it. As the idea fails miserably and predictably. As Chase gave up the idea of trying to go outside of the cell. He quietly sat on his bed and waited.

Chase did not really know what he was waiting for. But he just sat there in peace. Unbothered and untouched. As Chase tried to fade into deep sleep. Something stopped him. Something rare, but familiar. A force invisible of energy approached Chase. And heat waves came across Chase. As his vision became vivid and he felt dizzy and uncomfortable. He felt uneasy and unsafe. His back was ice cold, however he felt hot and heated.

The dizziness eventually got to him, and Chase fell on the ground and got into deep mental trauma.

"Hello?? Anyone here?" asked Chase

Chase looked around. Where he seemed to be in a container. Even though the background is pure black, he could still see an outline and a border.

"Hello...." said a deep voice.

"Yes. Hello" responded Chase

"Yes, I quite expected you. Um. You have someone dear to you who wants to visit." said the deep voice.

"Wait, hold on. You sound like Tony Musk."

"Um... I wasn't expecting you to notice this fast. But yes. I am the great Tony Musk." responded Tony Musk.

"Anyways, walk along the green tiles. And you shall meet him." continued Tony Musk.

"Ok. So we are just gonna skip the question that where is this place and why are you here." said Chase

"There is not enough time. Now move along." said Tony Musk.

Chase had more questions in mind, but for a lack of time he moved on. Chase saw a bright neon green flooring appear on the ground.

Chase followed the green flooring and eventually it led him to whom he thought he would never see again.

"Hello. Long time no see Chase." said a familiar figure.

"David is that you. Is that really you." asked Chase

"Yes. It is me in fact. We don't have enough time to discuss personal stuff yet. At least not yet." responded David

"Ok. So..." reacted Chase

"Yes. So I know you are trapped in a secret prison at the coordinates somewhere around -1567232, -99786123. Me and Tony Musk will try to get you out. However, we cannot do it through this dimension. We have to travel through another dimension to your and get you out. And I know there is an entrance to a dimension near you."

"How did you know?"

"We have a flowing system of communication. Lets say."

"Um. Ok."

"Yes. I shall continue. Um, we will try to open up a portal at my side."

"Ok. How are you going to do that."

"Um that's why we needed you here. So how did the portal appear the other day?"

"I don't know. I just woke up and saw this weird sphere."

"Um. That's gonna make our job much harder. So tell me what you did before you woke up."

"I had a weird dream. Well familiar place and people, but different."

"What do you mean different?"

"Well it's complicated. It all started..."

"No, I don't want to hear the whole thing. Just tell me what was different."

"Ok, um before that night. In that dream, I could not feel pain. However, that night. The same place, I felt pain. It was weird. I did not notice, because I was in a hurry."

"Alright. So you never felt pain in your dream. And after that incident the portal opened up."

"Yeah, I guess."

"Oh well. We might have a breaking point here. Um, anyways. Try to feel pain. If that makes sense. You have to go now. Time is up."

"Um..."

Before Chase could finish his sentence, he woke up in cold sweat. Chase shot right up from the table. Table... Table?!

Chase observed around and found himself in a different room. Bright neon white lights blast onto Chase's eyes. Cold metal table, which Chase is laying on.

Bare footed Chase made an effort to stand up. Chase felt weak. Arms sore, head pain, and a pair of unworking arms. With cold air blasting onto Chase's pale face.

As he was surrounded by medical tools, and large machines located to the west of Chase. Who was in the center of the room.

As in the corner of the room, a tube shaped machine turned. Chase focused on the object and noticed someone was watching him.

"Halle freind I notice you are awake. Yeas, I will callel the ductor." said a voice through a megaphone behind Chase that he still not realized that was there.

Chase sat there with disbelief of what just happened.

"Yes. Hello there. You are definitely awake, not dead. How are you feeling?" asked a figure with an awkward yet familiar costume.

"Wait, are you dressing like Kameron Mewton. And to answer your question I feel really weird." answered Chase

"Ahh yes. You know him. The Centerback. He played in the 2010's. Wow, that's old. How'd you know?"

"Um. Everyone knows that he dresses like trash. And you dress just like him. No offense." responded Chase

"No, I think he dresses pretty well. Well at least that's what my fashion designer told me. And I think he knows what he is talking about." as the figure pointed toward his head where an instant noodle was taped onto his head.

"Well, you should probably change to another fashion designer." suggested Chase.

"Anyways, let me call backup..."

## *The Phone Call...*

"Hello?? Yeah, he is not dead. Come help."

"Bee, bee, bee, boo?"

"Yes he is not dead."

"Dee, dee dade!""

"Yes. Send help."

"Digitada"

"Dadgummit. Yes, he is still alive. Send help."

"TIdi. BEEEEE"

"Yeah, help is on the wait. Yeah, in the meanwhile who's your favorite player in the UFL as in the Universal Football League? Not the old one on Earth."

"Um, it would probably be Optimus Prime."

"Ahh yes, Cxlvxn Jonathan. Yes, that guy. He is the best WR in the league. Mine would probably be Lamarcus Jackpot. One of the best Centerbacks in the league."

"Yes, I love the way he plays. His throwing and rushing stats. The way he jukes out opponents. And how he makes deep balls so seamless and easy."

The room was quickly fulfilled with emptiness. Nothing was left to do. As Chase looked onto the white tile floor. A triangle shape was nicely engraved onto the ground.

Creek... The sound filled the room as it echoed Chase's mind. As both of them looked toward the sound source. And was greeted with armed soldiers and medical practitioners.

"Where is the suspect?" asked one among the soldiers.

"He is here. He is actually exceptionally peaceful." said the creature that Chase had a conversation with prior.

"He is safe right now?" asked another among the soldiers.

"I am not entirely sure, but he seems fine right now. We did have quite a lovely conversation prior to your appearance."

"Now back off. We don't want any mortalities." said another soldier. Who Chase surmised was the commander of the group due to his goldenish and copperish badge on the right upper side of his pocket.

Chase stood there with confusion and apprehension. As the rest of the soldiers entered the small and crowded room, the closer the soldiers got.

BANG, BANG, BANG, BANG. The sound of gunfire was heard, medical helpers ran around and started screaming. Due to the chaotic environment, Chase fainted once again.

# CHAPTER 12

Pew, pew, vrooom. Pew, pew, pew. Gunfire was heard everywhere, people running around with fear in their eyes.

"Ahhh. RUN" screamed a random creature

"Mr. Musk, We can't hold them off longer. We have to move." reported David

"Have we got the child yet?" responded Tony Musk.

"I don't know, but we have to move!" said David.

"Go look for the child. I will hold them off." said Tony Musk.

David managed to stand up and moved toward the Castle of Famille royale d'Henri. Due to the destruction of the battle, there were places David could not go without the ability of flight. As in Tony Musks consideration, David was provided with an advanced adaptive analeptic suit. The suit has the ability of flight, protection from contact, heat, and acid. The suit also has a series of extensive weapons, such as two Heckler Koch MG43, one adaptive customizable laser rifle with a model similar to the AR-15, and more. The specialty about the adaptive suit and the laser rifle is the advanced technology that makes these stand out. One of the greatest inventions of all time hands down. The suit can make different responses and protection due to the environment. For instance, if the user is near fire the suit would make automatic adjustments to prevent fire from damaging the user. The rifle has automatic customized lasers that cause different things. The lasers change due to its environment and what it interacts with.

The suit has a nice design. The first layer is made from a mixture of strengthened aluminum and perfected stainless steel. This would protect the user from bullets, acid, and fire. The second layer is made purely from perfected Nitinol; which is the adaptive part of the armor. This particular piece will remember the form of its original build, which when damage is taken. It will still stay in the form of armor.

The final layer of the suit is made out of pure graphene combined with steel and the special material which David discovered in outer space. This piece of layer is very rare. With hundreds of hours to combine graphene with steel. However, due to the massive amount of resources and money Tony Musk has. They were able to create 10 of these, which they called the Armor Of the Star.

As David flew across the destroyed bridge, Tony Musk was not having a good time. The guards of the Empire were fiercely attacking the energy barrier. Tony Musk made a signal by talking into the armor, telling David to hurry up and get the child.

David had a difficult time navigating through the battlefield. Destroyed infrastructure, laser beams flying all over. And some shouting with anger, and some screaming with fear. David quickly scanned around the area.

With countless amounts of humanoid enemies on the right side. And with reinforcement on the left side. Time being little, David quickly confluced his countless thoughts and quickly ran toward the nearest entrance of Castle of Famille royale d'Henri. There was a tiny tunnel into the castle. However it was about 250 yards northwest from David.

This means David would have to cross the energy force barrier. This is potentially a fatal route to take. However, with little time to think. David quickly bolted toward the barrier.

David sent a quick signal to Tony Musk and asked for his opinion. However, there was no time to talk. David quickly ascended into the air about 20 feet. David zoomed across the barrier and flew across the crowd of enemies.

With some enemies following the trail of David. Tony Musk could still see the movement change. Tony Musk joined David's built-in voice call.

"What in the world are you doing??" asked Tony Musk.

"I need to get to the castle." responded David.

"Why didn't you tell me first?"

"There was no time. If I did not move, the child would have been gone."

"Fine. No time to argue. Anyways, I know the general direction of the child. Um it's about 500 yards of where you are going right now."

"Ok, I will head there right now."

"Be careful, call me if you need assistance."

David turbo boosted toward the direction. It caught more and more attention. More enemies are right on his trail. As some of them started shooting upon the sky. David had to make more effort to dodge the lasers.

Voom. Zoom. Veee. Left. Right. Left Right. As more and more enemies shot upon the sky. It was more and more difficult to dodge. David had no choice but to shoot down upon them. David is a real peaceful person. He would escape trouble if he could. However at this time, he had to blast hundreds of thousands 50000 degree lasers down upon. With screams trailing David, the enemies were distracted by the screams rather than David. This gave more comfortable space to fly. As David boosted more, leave the enemies far behind. He finally made a break for it. With a top speed of 146 mph, David managed to catch with no effort whatsoever.

As the area was immensely crowded, it was nearly impossible to locate where the child was with naked eye. However, with the help of a built in tracking system. Finding the carrier and the child was effortless.

The problem was there were drones flying upon the carrier twenty four seven. And also guards were behind and in front of the carrier at all times. This had David thinking, as he is not familiar with the environment of the battleground. And he has still yet to familiarize the entirety of the abilities the suit has. David is at his worst enemy yet. Unfamiliarity. Throughout his life, due to the unknown death of his brother, his main goal was to understand the world. At the small age of 3, he started immensely constantly learning and studying things around him. Now that he is 15, he had a pretty good understanding of what he had seen. However, this planet only drove him crazy. The gravitation, the creatures, and the physics behind the planet. This gets him afraid. As he has always been scared of the idea of not knowing. He thought bad omen and things would happen if he did not understand. As this gave him flashbacks of when his brother was killed.

### 5 Years Ago...

"GaHH." said Max, who was David's dead brother.

Booom. Purple lighting struck Max. As seconds later, a figure appeared behind Max's body.

"Um... Max are you *ok*?!" asked David in a shaking voice.

"My end is near. Tell Mom I love her. And tell Dad it was nev...er me...ant... t..o.. be ...." cried Max.

The figure behind Max, summoned dark energy which surrounded the room. And the dark energy formed as sharp knives.

"AHHHHHH!" shouted Max. Thousands of knives shot right into Max's back.

### Back to Presence.

David blinded in despair. As his eyes suddenly flashed, and his mind went back to presence. David shivered in freezing sweat, even though the suit itself adjusts to the most comfortable temperature. It wasn't his body that was cold. It was his mind.

Thinking about the arms of unknownness dragged him down into the freezing ocean of apprehension. As nothing could be done. A sudden flash brought David back to existence.

David was losing control of the suit.

As his mind needed a grasp of air. As the autopilot was turned on. David could finally have a peace of mind. As the sun or whatever this planet has is setting. Almost exactly the same as Earth, but something felt different. He felt weight on his shoulders. This was a brand new feeling. Before people had him covered. But this time, he is on his own. He looked into the sunset. Realized how things have changed, and people have to learn to adapt and change.

As David got his mind back to presence, the amount of enemies increased. The more of them were killed, a double was formed. As David noticed the change, he took control and turned around to check upon the state of the barrier.

It was not great, as they had been pushed several meters. Time was urgent, the barrier was almost pushed to an edge of a cliff, where most of Tony Musk's troops were. David tried to take the quickest route to the carriage. However, he could not get too low due to the enemies being comfortably close. David navigated through the numbers of skyscrapers. After about 2 minutes of navigation, the carrier entered a clear area. Where it's just plains everywhere, it was surprising how much green there was. The Urbanized areas were quite dry. David accelerated quickly, and as expected he was right below the carrier. The problem was taking the child. As the protection was crazy, if David was 10 feet closer, he would have been made into dust. As Tony Musk joined him in his voice call.

"How are you doing pal." said Tony Musk

"Um, no so great. I've caught up to them, but I can't quite figure out how to get the child." responded David

"What do you mean?" asked Tony Musk.

"I am about 200 meters above the carriage, but the guard near the carriage is nearly impossible to get near."

"Oh, I thought this would happen. Um I will send robot soldiers your way. Just send your direction."

As about 5 minutes passed, the robot soldiers arrived. They were ordered to attack the carriage. David joined in the middle. While the battle was going on David was planning to grab the child during the chaos.

As planned the robots dived head first onto the carriage. They were precisely programmed not to hurt the people in the carriage and to do the minimum damage.

"Ready, set, go." commanded David.

As ordered, two of the robots dived down, seconds later a group of 3 followed. Then another group of 2 followed. Seconds later, David joined them. As predicted the outer drones of the carriage detected the incoming. The drones shot lasers in their direction, due to how powerful the armor was, it did little to no damage. No robots were struck down.

Closer and closer to the carriage, the tighter and the more powerful the defense was. However in order for the mission to succeed, it had to be done. After the drones, personal guards started to shoot at the sky. The bullets were rapid, the armor could take the hits but it damaged the armor. David tried his best to dodge the bullets. Luckly, the robots would not be damaged. The robots took most of the hits. Each of the robots accelerated toward each of the guards. With the intention of blocking the view and the path of the guards, David planned to enter the carriage and obtain the child. The plan was simple but the execution would be difficult.

As there would be countless unanswered and time was urgent. Seconds passed, the closer and closer they were. David realized how unprepared they were. At that moment everything felt calamitous, fearsome thought kicked into his brain.

As the robots closed in, David prepared to blast off and obtain the target.

*"3, 2, 1. GO" signaled a robot.*

All of the robots were boosted and attached onto the guards. David blasts full power toward the carriage. David seconds later David was yards away from the carriage. To his surprise the robots did create a comfortable period where David could obtain the target. However, the robots could no longer hold on no longer. The guards have successfully shaked off the blocks of the robot. The guards were meters aways from David. David quickly grabbed onto the rails of the carriage. Kicked into the carriage and heard screaming. The Royal Family was there. David saw the queen screaming in fear. The king held onto the edge of the carriage.

David scanned the carriage. There it was. The child lay on the seat unprotected. David moved toward the direction. The King saw through David's purpose. The King grabbed onto David and cried for the rest of the family to protect the newborn and run. While David was being held on, the guards arrived. Kicking into the carriage. The fearless guards saw the presence of David. Quickly another guard appeared behind David unprotected back and tossed David out of the carriage; sending David 10 meters into the air.

However, David did not give up. He quickly gathered himself and dived back into the carriage and made another attempt to obtain the child. Again the guards were just too strong for David to handle. David activated combat mode. Forming a sword on top of his right arm. David slashed out the doors of the carriage. Being noticed, the guards shot laser beams at David. David blocked and dodged all of the shots.

David accerrated onward, meanwhile slashing his sharp blade.

"Ahhhh!" shouted David as he swung his blade onto a guard. The guard carelessly dropped onto the earth. With one down, there was one more in the carriage protecting the royal family. David formed a taser with his haptic armor and quickly shot a laser at the guard. With the guard asleep, the goal was to obtain the child quickly as possible. As more and more backups will be entering this battle. As the king, duke, and the prince were the ones who were left to defeat. The family was ready to fight, however they left the child unprotected and untouched. David's quick reaction time made him quickly grab the child and boost out of the carriage. Without realization David successfully escaped the danger zone. And he successfully completed the mission. According to plan, David and the remaining robots would fight 150 yards into the sky and there should be a flying ship for David to fly toward. David quickly descended from the situation, avoiding any attack in the carriage. The Royal Family would just powerlessly watch in desperation.

David regressed from the area , the remaining guards and drones started shooting at David. After the remaining guards noticed how useless their attack was, they quickly called for backup. Quickly, more and more enemies gathered below David.

# CHAPTER 13

"Hello?? Can you hear me?" asked a figure.

Chase unwillingly opened his tired eyelids. The bright light in the room prolonged the process. As Chase slowly but steadily unbarred his eyes. The sound of familiar murmuring.

"Uhh, what's happening." asked Chase

"Finally you are awake. After 20 hours, we thought you were dead." said the figure.

Rubbing his eyes, Chase took a few seconds to get back to consciousness.

Without thinking Chase shot right up. In an unfamiliar environment, Chase quickly scanned the surroundings.

A figure caught his eyes, a familiar yet a distanced figure With bright lights glaring, Chase could not work out who it was.

"Anyhow, do you want anything?" asked the figure

"Um, some water and some chips would be fine. Thanks" responded Chase.

"I will get you the water." said the figure.

The figure left the room quickly to get some water for Chase.

The familiar figure approached Chase.

"So how are you doing today Chase?" asked the familiar figure.

Chase made another attempt to figure out who this person was. However, he failed.

"Um, what's your name? Sorry." said Chase.

"Max, David's brother." responded Max.

"Yeah, that's why you looked familiar. Wait... Wait..." responded Chase

Chase looked toward Max. And remembered, David's brother died 5 years ago.

"Wait a minute. No disrespect but aren't you dead." continued Chase

"Um, what do you mean?" said Max. "Forget it. Anyways, would you explain the situation to me, please?" continued Chase.

"Ok. So, first you were in a freezer, I don't know particularly why. But a girl, claiming to be a close friend of yours, said that you somehow did a lot of damage and *they killed you?* I am not sure how that turned out. So then, we came and rescued you." said Max.

"Hmm. About the close friend, do you know who she is?" asked Chase

"Actually she is in the room next door. I think she is resting." responded Max.

"Yeah, I will talk to her later," said Chase.

Verrt. The door opened.

"Yes, I have gotten your water. And unfortunately we don't have chips. However, we do have some biscuits. Would you like some of that?" asked the figure.

"Just leave the water on the table, and yes get him some biscuits. Thank you Robert." answered Max.

Robert left the room.

"Yeah, take a rest, we will be serving lunch in about 40 minutes. And we are planning to meet up with Elon Stark within the next few days."

Max quickly left the room. Chase's mind was still somewhat confused, as so much has happened in a short amount of time. After Chase finished the biscuits, he looked for something to entertain and keep busy with himself. With nothing much in the room, he discovered a sheet of paper. An instruction paper of the things he could do in his room.

Chase quickly read through the sheet, and was surprised how many things he could do. With a command Chase could summon a TV, with things he could watch. With the ability to do that, Chase managed to keep himself busy.

As time passed, Chase faded into deep sleep.

"Long time no see Chase," said Faderion.

"Ahh, it's you again." said Chase

"Don't be so cold. Even though I almost killed you, doesn't mean we can't be friends. Right?" responded Faderion.

"Anyways, have you been training?" continued Faderion.

"No, many things have happened. I have absolutely no time whatsoever." said Chase.

"You know this for your own good. I think now that you are in a safe place. You should really build up your powers. You know Kerlis, the girl next door. Probably is more powerful than you." responded Faderion.

"Wait, Kerlis is here?" questioned Chase

"Yeah, did you not know? Oh right, you fainted." answered Faderion.

"Anyways, why am I here?" said Chase.

"Right, it's time for a test. To test your concentration level."

"Sure."

"Ok, I will summon some packaging peanuts and launch them at you. Your goal is to stop them. And if you pass that level, we will move up. And so on."

Chase remained silent. Suddenly, the room became darker. Chase positioned himself. And silently waited.

"Ready, set, go." shouted Faderion.

Chase could detect something in the far future. With the object going at 50 mph. Chase's objective was to stop it with telekinesis.

Seconds later, a vague view of the packaging peanuts soon appeared. Chase held up his arms waiting for the target to come closer. In a comfortable distance, Chase closed his eyes. His arms turned burning red, his skin tightened up, and his blood vessels accumulated toward his head. Even though Chase's eyes were dead closed, he still had a clear, if not a better view of the traveling object.

When the object was 50 yards away, it had slowed down. As it was easy to stop a 3 gram object. Chase struggled a little bit, due to the constantly moving and the smallness of the packaging peanut.

The packaging peanut was stopped about 47.5 yards from Chase. Due to how inconsistent Chase's practice is, Faderion considered this a solid score. However, it clearly showed Chase needed a lot more practice. As the average user of telekinesis can easily stop a packaging peanut hundreds of yards away.

Chase was quite disappointed at himself, he thought he was a lot more powerful than that.

"I see you did ok on that one. I can definitely see talent in you. You just need to practice." said Faderion.

"Anyways, it's time for you to go." continued Faderion.

Chase wanted to respond, however by the time he understood the sentence he was already back in the real world.

Chase slowly opened his eyes. Without hesitation, Chase jumped out of his bed. He quickly entered the bathroom. At least that was what Chase thought it was.

He was greeted with anothing. A blank area with nothing inside. Chase stared into space. Confusion flooded into his mind. He asked himself tons of questions and tried to figure out the purpose of the room. However, he had gone to the conclusion of asking for assistance.

Chase, unworried, walked out of the room. Looking for some kind of assistance.

Verirrt. Chase quickly looked to the left. Where a familiar figure happened to be looking out of the room.

"Oh hey kerlis." said Chase while he scratches his head.

"Good *morning?*" responded Kerlis in a confused voice.

"Where are you going?" asked Chase.

"Well, I was having some trouble with the bathroom." said Kerlis

"Ahh, yeah. I was just going to ask them how to use it." said Chase

"Oh, ok. Mind if I come with you?" requested Kerlis.

"Sure. I don't mind." accepted Chase

The two walked down the futuristic hallway. Then they entered the lunch area. And there who awaits them was Robert, the leading servant.

"Hey you two. What are you looking for?" asked Robert

"Hi, good morning Robert. We, well at least me, just woke up and wanted to use the bathroom. We did find a room with nothing in it." answered Chase

"Oh, yes! I did not explain the room to you. My apologies." said Robert.

"Please, follow me." continued Robert.

Chase and Kerlis followed Robert back into Chase's cabin. Robert quickly jogged near the room inside Chase's cabin and politely opened the door for Chase and Kerlis.

"Ladies first. Please!" said Chase as he sided with Robert.

"Thank you." responded Kerlis

Kerlis entered the room, then Chase, then Robert.

"Yes, ladies and gentleman. I shall begin showing how to access the bathroom." said Robert.

Chase and Kerlis stayed silent.

"Yes, this is the multiaccess room. It means that it's not just a bathroom. It can be countless different things. Such as a massage room, recording studio, mini movie theater, gym, shooting training area. And countless more." continued Robert.

"In order to access all of the rooms, you will need to do signals. And I will show you the basic signals." said Robert.

Robert walked out of the room into the bedroom. *Clap, Clap, Clap.* Robert calmly clapped three times.

"Good morning Robert, what can I do for you today." asked a female voice.

"Good Morning Stacy, would you give me the menu for the Multiaccess Room." responded Robert.

"Ok, request granted." said Stacy.

A 12 inch by 12 inch tablet slowly dropped down from the ceiling.

"Here it is, the tablet for the room." whispered Robert to himself.

"Ok, so these are the commands, for accessing the bathroom, you have to clap 5 times continuously without gaps. And the others are on this tablet. And in order to get the tablet just clap 3 times and request one from Stacy the AI." said Robert.

"Thank you Robert." said Chase

"Welcome, call me anytime you have questions," said Robert.

"Yeah thanks Robert," said Kerlis.

"And I will go back to my room now. Bye" said Kerlis

Instantly, she disappeared before Chase and Robert could respond.

Robert quickly left the room, leaving Chase by himself.

"Alright, let's get this over with." said Chase to himself.

After Chase used the bathroom, he exited his room and looked for food; as he had not eaten in 2 days. He came back to the lunch area, where Robert once was. Chase wandered around the area with the will to find food. Chase decided to do something new.

*Clap, Clap, Clap.*

*"How many I serve you today, Dear Chase."* responded Stacy.

"Hey Stacy, can you tell me where to get food? Thanks" said Chase

*"Food is not served until 7:30 East Universal Time. It is 5:46 East Universal Time. However, snacks can be served by Robert if needed."* said Stacy.

"Oh ok, understandable." answered Chase

*"Would you like me to call Robert for you?"* asked Stacy.

"Yes, please. Thank you." responded Chase.

*"Calling Robert."*

Moments later, Robert arrived at the lunch area.

"Yes Chase, you call for me?" asked Robert

"Yeah, I was wondering if I can have some snacks." said Chase

"Yes, of course. What would you like today? Hold on one minute. Let me get the menu" said Robert.

Robert struggled to pull something out of his bouch.

"Got it. Here you go." continued Robert.

Robert handed Chase a tablet which he assumed was the menu.

"Large variety of things," said Chase.

"Yes, for sure. What would you like today?" asked Robert.

"I would like a red velvet cake with matcha tea please." said Chase

"One red velvet cake and one cup of matcha tea coming up. Would you want me to bring the food to you?" asked Robert

"Yes please. Thank you." answered Chase

Chase left the lunch area back to his room. Hours later, Chase had finished the snack and was looking for things to occupy him.

Chase decided to train his abilities while he has time. Chase asked for an empty room, an apple, a book, a plastic cup and a gallon of energy drink.

With the room set up by robots, Chase could use the room within 5 minutes.

Minutes later, Chase entered the room, preparing for intense training.

With the room quite large Chase had the space to stretch out. Chase eventually started training in telekinesis. With an apple afar, Chase attempted to move it with telekinesis. Seconds later, Chase detected a shake in the distance. Though Chase wasn't really sure if the spaceship shook or Chase's attempt to use telekinesis. Without much time, Chase made another attempt to use telekinesis, this time Chase attempted to lift the apple up from the ground. With much concentration, a noticeable shake could be felt and observed. Chase continued the attempt to lift the apple up.

Seconds later, the apple made a forceful shake. Now Chase would really know it was him that moved the apple. With another push of force, Chase managed to get the apple levitate about 2 cm above. Seconds later, the apple fell back on the ground.

Chase walked around a bit, trying to recover his stamina, Chase reached out to the bottle of energy drink. However, a figure stopped him.

"Wait, you know drinking energy drinks will stunt your growth right?" said Max

"Uhh, I am 6 ft 2. I don't need to be taller." suggested Chase

"You are correct, but you know I am just saying" responded Max

"Yeah, why are you here?" asked Chase

"I was here to see what you were doing."

"Cool, I was just training in telekinesis." said Chase

"Oh! Telekinesis, that's interesting. The girl next to your room has teleportation."

"Yes, I know. Very useful power."

"What are you doing to train your power"

"I was trying to lift an apple off the ground. And it levitated for 5 seconds then it fell. I am kinda disappointed."

"No, I see this as an absolute win!" said Max.

Chase gave him a confused face.

"Really?" said Chase in a high pitched voice.

"Yeah, even though the achievement is not large, it still proves that you can do it."

Chase stayed silent.

"Anyways, I will go now."

Chase still had a suspicion of when Max avoided Chase when he was asked about his death.

"Um Max, I have a question." said Chase

Max stayed silent.

"Yeah, what happened to you? David and us thought you were dead."

"David? My dead little brother?!"

"Huh? What do you mean?"

"I don't know what you are talking about, but from what I know, I am not the one dead, and we are supposed to meet up with Elon Stark in about 2 days."

"Wait, did you say Elon Stark?"

"Yeah, Mastermind, Quintillionair, Ladies' Man, and humanitarian"

"Yes I know, but isn't his name supposed to be Tony Musk?"

"Nah, from what I remembered it's Elon Starks. Look I'll even look it up for you."

"Hey Stacy, what's the name of the Mastermind, Quintillionair, Ladies' Man, and humanitarian?" continued Max

*"Showing results for "Mastermind, Quintillionair, Ladies' Man, and humanitarian" Dear Max, I think you are trying to describe Tony Musk."* answered Stacy.

"Wait, nonono." said Max

"I told you, it's Tony Musks."

Suddenly, Max's upper body stretched away from his lower body. Within a split second, everything went back to normal.

"Nononono" said Max as he looked at his hand.

"What's wrong?" asked Chase

"*Everything...*" said Max in a shaking manner.

Coldness crowded up Chase's veins. Chase could feel the room temperature drop. Max's body began to violently shake.

"Are you alright?" asked Chase as he placed his hand on Max's shoulder.

"*No, no, no. I need to go...*" cried Max and he busted out the door.

With confusion deep inside Chase, he was baffled by the situation. Chase wanted to sprint after Max, but something told him it was not the right time.

Chase froze in space as more and more confusion kicked in his plain mind. Without much thought, Chase quickly got back to training. Wanting to give Max some time and space.

Moments later, Chase got on with his day. The day quickly passed and nothing special really happened.

The next day was the last day until they would meet Tony Musk. Chase felt it was time to confront Max, and try to understand what was happening. After Chase's telekinesis training, Chase found his way to Max's bedroom.

Minutes later, Chase arrived at the entrance.

*Knock, Knock.*

"Who is it?" shouted Max

"It's me. Chase" responded Chase

"Oh, come in.."

With the permission to go in, Chase was a bit scared. Quickly, Chase gathered himself, and entered the room. Where he meets a relaxed Max.

"Hi, Chase. What are you doing here?" asked Max

"I came here to talk about yesterday." Chase responded calmly.

"Yes, about that. Come, sit down."

Chase walked across the room, where a seat was placed.

"Now, let's talk." suggested Max

"Yeah, why did you run off yesterday?" asked Chase

"Ok, for you to understand this, you would have to understand the situation."

Chase stayed silent.

"This might seem absurd, but there is a thing called multiverse. You see, I was on the exact same mission that I am now. To meet up with Elon Stark."

"*Ok?*"

"I was on my way to the destination. However, this is when things go wrong. You see, at that time, I was resting. The ship was on autopilot. I was not aware of the situation at first. The ship entered a wormhole. A wormhole, in which enters your universe."

"So you entered a wormhole, which took you to my universe?! That is quite hard to believe."

"I know it is, but trust me. There is a very concerning question that has not been answered yet. Who opened up the wormhole?"

"Why does that matter?"

"You see, wormholes don't appear by themselves. It is formed by a powerful source of energy."

"......"

"You see, in my universe wormholes were banned a long time ago. With the intention of forbidding illegal transactions, and marking the territory of our universe. And the Universal Alliance decided to thicken the border, making it almost impossible to enter or leave without a citizenship, or visitor card."

"Ok? Keep going."

"You will need so much force and power to open an illegal wormhole. This is what is concerning me. Something that powerful exists in the universe and it is looking like it's not here for good."

"But, we still need further proof to get help from the Alliance."

"You see, the alliance is definitely hiding something from us. I am not sure the reason, but I am sure it will frighten the people once leaked. And if we get the secret information, we might not be safe."

"Ok, I get what you are coming from. But we will need much help if we want to find out what the secret is."

"Yes, I know. I am still trying to plan the next step. But, keep this between you and me."

"Understood."

"Alright, prepare now. We have under 14 hours until we meet up with Elon Star.... Tony Musk."

Chase silently exited the room, hoping things are not as bad as they might be. However, he was dead wrong.

# CHAPTER 14

"David, ya there?" asked Tony Musk

"There are quite a lot of enemies here, help sound nice right now." accepted David as he dodged a bullet.

"Yeah, I am flying toward the destination." responded David

"You need help?" offered Tony Musk

"Alright, 15 more robots coming your way."

With help coming the way, David was more assured. Moments later, several robots arrived by David. Waiting for David to give command. David, being reasonable, orders some of the robots to temporarily put them to sleep. With the rest to protect himself and the unconscious royal-blooded child. From the assistance of the robots, David was quickly able to safely leave the battlefield. Without bullets coming from below, it became murderously quiet. David's thoughts began to enter his mind.

These thoughts were not particularly pleasant. But David was forced to move on as he became unconsciously near the spaceship.

"Would you mind opening the entrance for me?" asked David

"Yeah sure." responded Tony Musk.

*"Access Accepted"* showed up on his inside screen. A large entrance opened up.

David, who had never done this before, struggled quite a bit. After a few failed attempts, he was able to set foot on the deck.

He entered the spaceship, where he was met by a sign.

*Place your hand on this sign to enter.*

*As* the instruction said, David placed his hand on the sign.

As soon as his hand was placed, a mechanical arm popped out of the ground, and absorbed his suit. Now, David was able to enter the spaceship.

"Hello David, welcome aboard. " said an artificial intelligence.

David did not have the stamina to respond. Instead, he went deeper into the spaceship. In search of Tony Musk, he found himself entering the cockpit of the spaceship.

With the anticipation to see Tony Musk, instead he was greeted with a mysterious creature. It was a humanoid, about 9 feet tall, and with unusual physique parts. A massive wing on its back, supernaturally large claws on its hand.

The creature stared at David. Seconds later, David's eyes sparked with fear and confusion. The creature made a sudden movement, then rushed toward David. In the creature's eyes, the will of killing blazed. David quickly ran the other way, as he noticed the creature had the intention to kill.

David was defenseless against this ruthless creature. The only solution was to run, as this was the only way he could possibly survive.

*Bang, Bang, Bang, Bang. Clank, Bang, Clank.* The sound of metal being smashed was all David could hear. The hallway was simply too small for the creature to fit in.

With the size advantage, David could get to places a lot easier than the creature. However, due to the unreal height and leg muscles the creature has. The creature could easily outrun David.

With the mass destruction the creature has made, the robots are soon alerted. With the crew of the spaceship arriving at the situation. This gave David more time for escape.

David thought of a plan, it's simple yet dangerous. The uncertainty is huge, and it's the only way David could think of.

David quickly turned right, going in the direction of the spaceship entrance. The only way for protection and survival. David kept running hoping for the right timing. However, the creature does not seem to slow down. Everywhere David goes, the sound of metal being bashed.

David noticed that the robots on the ship are actually trying to slow the creature down. One tried to electrocute the creature, however this only seemed to increase the power of the creature.

David made another turn, entering the lunch area. David struggled to get across, due to the mass amount of water on the ground. However, the creature seemed to struggle even more. It seemed water was doing damage to the creature. It had drastically slowed down the creature. Which was a perfect opportunity to execute the plan.

As David exited the lunch area, while the creature was still restrained from the water. As David comes close to the entrance of the spaceship. He was planning to activate the suit and hopefully stand a chance against the roughless creature. However, the loud noise that was produced made David think on his toes. With not much support, he only had one chance. And it had to be perfect.

Quickly entering the entrance, suddenly the spaceship became murderously quiet. David drastically slowed down, as the silentness deeply frightened him.

Consequently, David somehow wanted the noise of destruction to come back. As he does not further understand the situation. And guesses slowly emerged into David's mind.

The unsureness sabotaged David's plans. He was unsure what to do. His mind was stunted by the silentness, and could not operate. As the silentness continues, David finally was brought back to reality.

He quickly pressed the button, which activated the suits. As soon as the button was pushed, the creature appeared again and jumped in the direction of David looking to make the final attack.

However, his attack had been blocked. David successfully entered the suit and was able to block the hit on time.

The creature was surprised, as his hit was blocked. While the creature was still in amazement, David made a powerful counterattack.

David slid toward the right, and made a hurtful punch right at the creature's face. To David's surprise, the punch was able to do a decent amount of damage to the creature. The creature was knockbacked by about 7 feet. As the monster struggled to get up, David landed another hurtful punch at the creature. This was able to knock the creature dead onto the metal surface.

In rage, the monster unexpectedly jumped right up and hit David. The punch hit right at David's stomach, knocking him 8 feet off the ground. Even though the suit reduced lots of the damage, David could still feel drastic pain from the punch.

To the creature's surprise, David was able to survive the hit. As the creature went for another hit. David was able to activate a tool which could destroy the creature in one blow.

An enhanced elemental gun, a weapon in which could blast out the basic four natural elements. In which included fire, water, lightning, wind, and earth. One of the elements was the creature's weakness. David was able to pull out the gun in time to save himself.

He blasted a gallon of water at the creature.

"Ah Gggg" the creatures screamed in pain.

David used the opportunity to quickly back away from the creature. The creature blindly rushed toward David attempting for another attack.

Even without eyesight, the creature barely missed. Missing by and quarter of an inch to the left arm of David.

David quickly backed away, in which he bumped onto the wall. He could no longer back away. David countered with another blast of his gun. However, this time the creature was no longer hurt by the water.

The creature simply deflected the water back toward David. It quickly countered with a punch right on his stomach. The creature managed to get hold of David. David was trapped and had nowhere to go. The creature ripped David's protective helmet off. Before the creature could attack again, David was able to escape the helm of the creature. David quickly dodged sideways. However David accidentally tripped on one of the wires of the ship. The creature suddenly stepped toward David and made an attempt to punch him.

This time, David was defenseless against the creature. Nothing could save him now. Without anyone around being able to protect him, doom was awaited for him. Suddenly, everything seemed to slow down. It seemed like death itself was taunting him. Death was slowly yet surely coming toward him. Yet he could do nothing about it. The dreadfulness was truly horrifying and torturing. Each millisecond passed by, it seemed to move by a centimeter.

# CHAPTER 15

To the left of Chase, a standup window was placed. A loud noise was heard to the left of him. With the expectation to see planes, nothingness of the universe. At first Chase could not believe what he saw.

Several hundred space jet fighters, pointing directly at their own spaceship. All the space jets had a similarity, they all had a logo. A large rose, with a shape of a bullet on it.

Chase recognised the logo, he had seen it somewhere. Though he did not know where and when. However there was no time to think.

Suddenly, the space jets started firing at the spaceship. Millions of lasers were shot in a second. One came near Chase, then dozens suddenly flew in. Fortunately, Max's spaceship was durable enough to hold up most of the attacks.

However, it was not unbreakable. Dozens of seconds passed, the spaceship automatically entered self-defense mode. Windows were closed off by strong metal, and the spaceship was covered by protective material that could protect the people on board for a while.

Chase rushed on the main deck, searching for others. One familiar figure appeared in the same room. Kerlis appeared at the main deck. Also looking for others.

"Kerlis are you ok?" asked Chase

"Fortunately, I am currently fine. Do you know what's happening?" responded Kerlis in a confused tone.

"No not really, we should probably go find the others" suggested Chase

Kerlis nodded in agreement.

Chase and Kerlis went down the closest hallway that was near them.

Opening and closing each and every day, trying to find others. However, nobody could be found in any of the rooms. Then they went into another hallway. Eventually, they stumbled into a familiar figure.

Gordom, who was once Kerlis and Chase's cellmate. The figure in which cannot be killed or harmed. The person has immortality but one who does not seek and desire it.

"Hey guys, what are you looking for?" asked Gordom

"We need to get out of here. There are a bunch of enemy spaceships blasting lasers at us." responded Chase in a hurry.

"What are we waiting for? Let's go!" suggested Gordom.

"Yeah, we need to find Max." added Chase

With the now formed squad, searching for the owner of the spaceship, the process became a lot faster. Soon, they found Max. The unworried owner, carelessly walked around, seemingly waiting for something.

"Max! There are a bunch of enemies shooting at us. What should we do?" asked Chase

"Much worry is not needed. I have a plan. And it will be perfectly safe." responded Max in a calm voice.

"No seriously, there are close to hundreds of thousands troops waiting outside." responded Kerlis.

"Yes, I understand. I have a plan." said Max

"Was your plan to escape with the mini spaceship in the back of this?" asked Kerlis

"Yes... How did you know? And even if they did see us escape with it. There would be no way they would catch up. I mean it's 15 times faster than light." responded Max

"Yeah, it won't work. That spacecraft was destroyed about 20 minutes ago." said Kerlis.

"Huh? Sorry, what? I could not hear you correctly." said Max

"No, what you heard was exactly what I said." responded Kerlis

Silence, the dismayed look on Max's face worried everyone. Max stared into space searching for a plan of survival. His eyes were blinded by nothingness. As they were desperate to find a solution. Suddenly, Max's eyes sparked.

"I got it, but I am not one hundred percent that it will work." said Max

"I know that all of you have some kind of supernatural powers. And to all of your surprise I have one too." continued Max

Everyone stayed silent.

"Though I am not quite as efficient and effective as some of you. I do know how to use it." said Max

"Ok, tell us what your power is?" asked Gordom.

"Yes, I can travel through time and space. Basically, I can travel to any point of time, and anywhere. But here it is, I can't bring many people with me." answered Max

"Continue." said Kerlis

"At my current state of skill, I can't use it often." added Max

"And also, this is really uncertain. We might be teleported to ancient times, or end up hundreds of trillions of light years away." continued Max

"But can it get us out of here though?" asked Gordom

"Yes, it definitely can. But one has to be left behind." responded Max

Silentness quickly filled the room after everyone acknowledged the fatal issue. After minutes of silence, Gordom stepped out.

"I volunteer to be the one." said Gordom in a confident voice.

"What? To be left behind? No, we are not leaving anyone behind." objected Chase.

"Well it's the only. I am physically invincible. They can't possibly kill me. Even if they can, I beg them to do it." reassured Gordom.

Chase and Kerlis understood Gordom's pain. Living alone for more than 500 years. Not really having someone close to him, and seeing everyone around him die.

# CHAPTER 16

When the skies were blue, flowers were blooming. Gordom was a regular being. Living in the arms of happiness and enjoyment. However, as time went on, things went very wrong.

A large storm rolled by that night. An unforgettable, unbelievable, and tragic night was soon to occur.

At sunset, everything seemed normal as everyone was at the usual. However, something changed drastically. Hours passed after sunset, a strange object could be seen gently gliding across the horizon. It was a dim yet visible sighting.

Though it was visible no one really paid much attention to it. More people had come back into their homes from their day. As for Gordom, he had just come back from his high school. After he arrived home, nothing really happened.

It soon became midnight, with nothing particularly happening. Though that was soon to change.

*Verrrrrt, Verrrrrrt, Verrrrt. Booooom.* Sounds of bombing suddenly occurred in the middle of the night. With unknown intentions, the citizens were forced to exit the areas of bombing.

Fortunately many were able to escape. However, Gordom was not one of them. A bomb landed right on top of their house. In which Gordom was in the attic at the time, which hit directly at him.

Boooom! After the loud noise was heard, everything went black.

Hours later, everyone who was able to escape assumed Gordom was dead.

A bright light shined through the rime of the debris that had cascaded upon him. Unfortunately, several amounts of fair sized debris had fallen on him, which led him to the inability to move at the moment. Gordom was unsure if he would ever be able to move again, as he could not feel the entirety of his left arm, which was buried under a large piece of an unknown material that had previously fallen and crushed him.

Although he was alive, he had vague memories of what just happened. He tried his absolute best to remember what had happened. However nothing came to his mind at that point.

Several hours later, filled with boredom and desperation, Gordom finally managed to regain some strength. He was able to move his right arm a bit. A scent of bright hope flourished. A bright light of faith shined through the callous debris that was above Gordom

Everything seemed the brightest until it wasn't. The laminating scent of hope was quickly wiped off as it revealed itself. And the bright lights of faith were darkened by the truth.

Another bomb landed right next to Gordom. The feeling of hope turned into a feeling of hatred and despair.

As a clear countdown clock winded down. It seemed like it was teasing Gordom. Slowing yet surely killing him, but he could not do anything about it. As his life seemed to slip away, he saw something. Something that would soar his hatred. It was a logo, a logo that everyone in his town would recognize, and have the same reaction as Gordom's. It had a peace sign on it, with an outline of a sun around it. It was the sign of the Universal Peace Organization. The exact organization that was helping Gordom's town. However there was another logo that Gordom did not recognize. A rose with a bullet shape inside of the rose.

As he was confused, and disappointed in the corruption of the truth. However, there was no time to think. Nor warn the others. As his own life was slipping away second by second.

He did not think much about his 15 years of life. Nothing particularly occurred in his short time. His family was no different from others. Though he rarely got to see his father. As work has kept the father and son relationship far and strange. His siblings were always annoying in his eyes. However as of now, he learned to accept and precious their relationships. However, it was too late for that realization.

As he prepared for his final end, a beam of bright light blasted into his face. He could not figure out whether he was in heaven or still alive. A figure appeared in the far distance, slowly the figure became closer and closer to Gordom. The figure shined a great source of blinding light. Soon enough, the figure was feets away from Gordom.

"My child, it is perhaps too soon for you to leave this cruel world. The greater ones have a lot more planned for you. It may be harsh and crushing, but please bear with it." said figure in a calming voice.

"God, is that you?" asked Gordom as he kept one of his arms up to dodge the blinding light.

Without a response, the figure seemed to let something go out of his hands. A flowing source of blue light slowly floated toward him. It went straight into his chest. Gordom felt something, strength and power. The blue ball of light seemed to give him power. He felt refreshed and seemed to have been reborn into another.

"There my child. Now go back to that world and do what was planned." said the figure. Suddenly, he saw multiple figures beside him. Them all being sent back down to the world.

Then Gordom fell, fell deep into the real world.

"Ahh!" cried Gordom.

He found himself on top of a large pile of debris. It seemed like an explosion. No matter what happened, Gordom survived the bombing. Confused, yet amazed. However, Gordom had to escape the collapsed building he was in. As more of the debris started to crumble.

Darkness soon occurs, and coldness soon to enclose. Gordom had felt fatigue, his entire body felt heaviness as he was desperate to fall and rest. However, he could not as if a thousand birds pulled against his urge to rest.

As after the strange encounter with whoever it was, Gordom was still baffled by what just had happened.

Despite having extreme tiredness, Gordom was forced by something to keep going.

In front of Gordom was a pile of debris that had piled up easily over 45 feet. With the remaining strength Gordom has left. He was sure he would not be able to go over.

Suddenly, a large piece of concrete fell upon Gordom. Fortunately, it did not hit Gordom.

MInutes later, Gordom was about to escape the former apartment of he and his family. Seconds after he had safely exited the building, the whole building collapsed.

Tons of steel and concrete fell right before Gordom's eyes. The place where he and his family lived for over a decade. All of the precious memories fall right before his own eyes. A scent of woefulness and pain merged in the air. Though he never realized how precious the apartment was, it had now fallen before his own very eyes. He never realized the details, though now it is very much gone. He took the apartment for granted. Never appreciate the importance and the meaning behind the emotionless building. However, now is too late to appreciate what he had. It was all gone.

Though the collapse of his former house, deeply scared him. Gordom had to keep going. He was unsure what would happen to the area.

Right there, Gordom realized the meaning of life.

People take things for granted. Never realizing how their life would be different without it. How the meaning was overlapped by the worth. How, people are blinded by the worth rather than the true meaning. Until it's demolishment, people will never understand the true meaning of it.

Gordom soon exited the area. He went into the nearby forest. Hoping to find a shelter and hopingly have some rest. As he went deeper into the forest, the blurrier his vision became. His body had needed rest, the blast had got the most of him. His body felt heavy. As heavy as guilt of murder on a broken soul.

Soon enough, his body had stopped working. Gordom fell right on the ground. With the little vision he had left, he saw a figure. Slowly making its way toward Gordom. Heavily armed men, with deadly weapons. Vaguely he saw a sign on the left shoulder of the figure. A rose with a bullet shape inside.

Gordom was unconscious for an uncountable amount of hours. At first the people around thought he was dead most of the time. All Gordom could remember was the armed men taking him away.

"AHhhhhhh!" screamed Gordom, as he woke up in cold sweat.

Gordom was surrounded in darkness. He had no idea where he was, and how he was still alive.

Surprisingly, Gordom was on a mattress. A quite comfortable mattress. Gordom decided to explore around. He slowly got out of bed.

It was the first time in months that he had walked. It was quite an awkward situation, as he had no idea why he could not walk properly. He felt like a newborn again. However, he managed to lean against the wall. The room was completely dark, nothing was visible until you got close.

After walking forward for a few meters, he saw a scent of light. A dim source of light coming below. Gordom carefully walked toward it. He was unsure of what was under the wooden board that was covering the light source. Fighting the urge to uncover the light. Gordom cautiously opened the cover. Unraveling the room below.

The sharp light had momentarily blinded Gordom. Gordom had no idea why this is, as he had no idea that he had been asleep for 3 months. The absences of light during the three months, had he fatigued by the sharp source of light.

Gordom slowly forced himself to open his eyes. For some reason Gordom was not blinded by this, as some people could possibly be permanently blinded. After a few minutes of adjusting to the light, Gordom was able to barely see. He saw a decaying ladder leading down to the room below. With little vision and strength, he was barely able to set foot on the steps. With much wobble, caution had to be taken. As the depth of the ground was quite high from where Gordom was.

The ladder seemed very old, some of the screws were borderline nonexistent. There was also much dust on its steps. However, silhouettes of activity were visible. With an outline of a hand here and there. With also lots of outlines of shoes on the steps.

A few steps later, Gordom was able to jump down onto the ground. Gordom turned a corner, and there he was met by an immense amount of light. It blinded him for minutes, though his presence was in the room. And he had temporary blindness, he was just standing there. It seemed like there was no one with Gordom right now.

Minutes later, Gordom's vision slowly recovered. With the expectancy to see high tech lasers guarded by robots. It was quite the opposite.

Suddenly, the gusts of the warm wind started blowing. With a wholesome fireplace on the far right side of Gordom. The whole room dispensed a feeling of warmness. Gordom was quite confused, he was sure the armed men had taken him away. And he was sure it was not for good. However, he ended up in a quite nice place. Something had him guessing, he was sure it was an illusion. There was no way whoever captured would treat him this nicely. The room was not big, however it was a manageable space.

For some reason, this place seemed like somebody's house. But no, Gordom thought he must not be fooled by the situation. No matter how real things might be, he must have a clear mind.

Gordom continued to walk around the room. Being cautious wherever he went and whenever he was. Minutes passed, nothing had happened. Suddenly, the walls started creaking. On the right corner of the room, a small part of the wall started retracting into itself. Gordom quickly helps up a pen in case things get brutal.

And there stood a figure. A young woman about 17 appeared at the secret door way. Wearing jeans and a t-shirt with a leather jacket overlapping it. With a fit figure, the woman was quite slim.

Gordom was quite surprised. As he was confused why whoever captured him sent a young woman to check on him.

"Hey, who are you and where am I?" yelled Gordom

"Oh god, ohh. Um, I am not here to harm you." stuttered the woman.

"I am here to help you." continued the woman.

Gordom was confused.

"Prove it" said Gordom while he held out the pen.

"You see you were captured by the RoseLaFire. A universal criminal organization, who goes around for creatures with supernatural abilities. And using them in the name of justice. " responded the woman

"Luckly, before they brought you far. I defeated the armed people and rescued you." continued the woman

"What supernatural powers? I don't have any superpowers, why would they go after me?" asked Gordom

"How did you think you survived the bombing?" responded the woman.

"I am not particularly sure what your power is, but I am sure it is very powerful. Because there were about 12 armored trucks. Just to transfer you." continued the woman.

"Who are you?" asked Gordom

"Oh wait. Sorry, forgot to introduce myself. My name is Scarlet. Nice to meet you. I am the one who has been keeping you alive for the past few months." responded the Woman.

"Huh? Months? What are you talking about?"

"Right, I forgot. After you receive your power. You will be unconscious for about 3 to 4 months."

"Wait what! What's your power?"

"Mind Manipulation, basically I can put people in an illusion."

"Wait, who gave me my power?"

"It should be the Outer World. A man, but you can't see his face. And in the end he sends a ball of light into your chest."

"Ohhhhh, I met that person."

"Did he say anything to you?"

"He said something like, it's too soon for you to go."

"Oh ok, so you are destined to do something great."

"Sorry?"

"If he said something to you, it means you are destined to do something great; you are basically one of the protagonists. If he doesn't but still sends you the ball of light, he is basically the supporting character. But if he doesn't appear at all, then it means you will do something great but extremely evil."

"Um, Ok?"

"But let me warn you. Be extremely careful out there. Remember, those people are still looking for you. If you are not with us, I cannot help you."

"Alright, then I will be leaving soon now."

"No, do not. Out there it's just a bunch of wasteland. And there are lots of criminal civilizations out there. We will let you have your personal time. But you still need time to recover."

"What do you mean by we?"

"I am actually in an organization. ProtectorTurquoise, a personal organization to help and protect the ones with supernatural powers."

Scarlet quickly scrambled a badge out of her jacket. It said "Project PT", with a Universal Union Stamp on it.

"Hmmm."

"Trust me, we are not here for bad. I am here to protect you."

"Wait, so are there more people like me here?"

"Yes there are more survivors that I brought here. I'll introduce you to some of them later. But first you need to eat."

"No, thank you."

"No, you need it. It seems to have a special ability. I'll make some healing pills that will help you tremendously."

"Ok, that would be nice. Thank you."

"For now, just relax on the couch."

Gordom was still quite surprised at what just had happened. As very much he had no idea what Scarlet was talking about.

Minutes passed, the healing pills were ready. It had a light scent of cherry blossom and mint.

Scarlet set the bowl on the table and quickly left.

After Gordom had finished the pills, he started walking around the place. Expecting to see some high tech gear. It was nothing but a bunch of furniture. Without much point to walk around, he returned to what seemed to be the living room.

And there he was met by something unexpected. Something that is extremely deadly without help.

# CHAPTER 17

Aflash gone by, expecting his life to slowly fade away. However, he was thrown across the room by an unknown force.

And there appears Tony Musk, with an arm extending seemingly thrown both the monster and him across the room.

Though David once again slimy slipped away from death's hug. David was heavily thrown into the complex world of pipes, he was fortunate to escape death. But he was deeply injured. The pain was like a million little blades had cut through his back.

As it seemed the same for the creature, though he was very much sure that he took much much more damage than the creature. With much pain, it was impossible for him to even attempt to stand up.

Tony Musk calmly walked toward the creature. With a taunting stance, he lifted the creature with a single hand. With over a ton on his hand, he threw the creature forcefully toward the entrance of the engine room. Tossing over a ton of weight effortlessly over at least 30 feet.

The creature was unconscious, with much chaos over. David had still had difficulty standing up. As he was sure, some of his legs and back bones were completely crushed.

Even though Tony Musk was able to defeat the creature. It seemed that he took some damage too. As the arms of his armor were slightly damaged. And he seemed to be tired.

"Ahhhhhh, ow, ow, ow. Mr. Musk, would you mind helping me up?" cried David.

"Yeah sure, sorry about that." responded Tony Musk.

"Things seem to get chaotic when I don't control myself." continued Tony Musk.

"How did you do that? I am sure the creature is over one ton." asked David

"Well, I'll tell you about that later. We need to get your injuries fixed up." said Tony Musk.

Tony Musk lends a hand to David, slowly lifting David up. Setting him on his back, slowly carried him back into the medic station.

With the creature still to deal with. Once David was set in the medic station, he went back to deal with the dying corpse of the creature.

David was instructed to sit in the wheelchair that was near the entrance of the medic station. With the only instruction, David was quite confused about what to do next.

Suddenly, a set of unknown material strapped David onto the wheelchair. With his hands and feet unable to move, he was dead locked onto the chair. The wheelchair started moving by itself. It made its way into a large tube of some kind that was able to fit it and David. With the wheelchair making most machinery noises, a net of lasers slowly came down.

The laser soon approached David, the laser slowly went through David. Seemingly scanning the injuries he endured. A few seconds later, the wheelchair made its way out of the tube. Settling onto an open area, the wheelchair started to transform. The footrest was kicked up slowly, and the backrest started calmly setting backwards. The Armrest was completely retracted into the seat. After it was completely made into position, numbers of cushions appeared making the seat more comfortable.

Now David was in a tilting position, ready for the next procedure. A few moments later, it seemed like the scanning results were finished.

It had successfully determined what medical attention in which David should receive.

The wall behind David started changing. A large part of the wall was retracted into itself, revealing a large machine. It was a half circled machine, with a number of mechanical hands on its side.

Slowly, the wheelchair backed into the machine. The wheelchair made a beep sound and the wheelchair attached itself to the machine.

"By the leg the Patient has a completely non-existent Hamstring. Torn Achilles. With the leg bone shaft completely shattered, Hip Bones crushed, Patella badly squished, and more bone tissues are destroyed. By the back, the spinal cord is not working correctly. The spine being horrifyingly cracked. By the arm, minor muscle torn, and some bones disconnected. Surgery should have a hundred and ten percent success rate. And approximately one hour to complete." said the medical machine.

Without much disturbance, the machine started the procedure.

An hour later, the procedure was done, even though it was a long period. David was all healed up. After the surgery, he had some minor pain in his back and legs. Walking was quite awkward, as his entire leg was crushed. Most of his injuries were fixed up, however there was something he could not do. Being able to easily move this pinky. This could easily fix up, but David did not want to bother.

David left the medic station after another scan. He went to look for Tony Musk as he was unsure what to do next. Moments later, he heard the familiar voice of Tony Musk. A door had a slight crack, with more than one voice inside.

At first David wanted to knock and come in, however David heard something suspicious. He decided to eavesdrop for a bit.

"Next time be careful though, the kid is important to the plan." murmured a voice, who seemed to be Tony Musk.

Another voice spoke. It seemed to be an alien language. David had no idea what it meant. But he was one hundred percent sure it was not a human.

"I understand, but I believe you have to leave now."

David had to scramble quickly, as the conversation was over. After David had arrived into this room, he was confused. He was unsure of who and what Tony Musk was talking with. Suddenly, Tony Musk entered the room. Seemingly to check up on David's injuries.

"How are you doing David?" asked Tony Musk

"Well, the surgery was a success but I have to get used to walking again." responded David.

"Well, that's good. I'll let you rest." said Tony Musk

David did not want to speak on the conversation he had heard between Tony Musk and whoever. David did not think much of this, however in the back of his mind, he definitely had some suspicion. He wanted to further investigate, even though Tony Musk showed nothing but kindness and help, David still did not one hundred percent believe him. David was told to rest after the surgery as it would help get used to the fixed up wounds.

Hours later, David had just woken up from his sleep. Without much disturbance, David was able to get a healthy amount of rest. The back and leg pain was not as painful as it once was. However, it had still sabotaged his ability to move swiftly.

Suddenly, a bright flash of light sparked in front of his mind. Seconds later, he appeared in another setting. He was teleported to where he is now. It was pitch black, with just a slight amount of light, that was able to make the area hardly visible. David felt dizzy in an instant. It felt like his head was a bottle of soda being shaken violently. It seemed like it would explode any second by now. With immense pain, suddenly the surroundings changed again. Before David realized, he was free falling in the sky. Without much thinking, David flipped over seemingly using the surface mass of his body to slow him down.

As the lower he got, the slower he seemed to fall. Moments later, the ground was feet below. Right at the moment David was about to hit the ground, he fell on the soft clouds hundreds of feet above.

With much surprise, David slowly got up. The head pain was no more. He actually felt quite the opposite, delight and comfort. David slowly adjusted his eyes to the bright light. Moments passed, a glowing figure appeared. The figure seemed to be in a sitting position. The figure was covered with glowing gems. It also had a dark blue crystal on the center of its forehead.

David slowly approached it. With just about 10 feet between them. David froze, he was unable to move. Suddenly, the figure stood up. It gracefully floated toward David. The figure landed a head in front of David. Still gracefully floating on air.

"What a beautiful set of eyes." said the figure.

The figure raised its hand, gently placed it on David's right cheek. David tried to pull away, however he was frozen in air. He could not move, but to watch. However, he found out he was able to talk.

"Who are you and what do you want?" cried David.

"Oh, little prince can talk. Haha." said the figure

"To answer your question, I am a member of Made In Heaven. You may know what it is." continued the figure

"Made In Heaven?! What?! The myth of the bloodline of the outer world. I thought it was just a legend." said David.

"Hmmmm, who said it was a legend? Exactly, my purpose here is to inherit my blood and mark you. So that in the future, I can relive in the form of you. I am on the near bridge of death. And eventually my blood in you will mature. And I will reform in the form of your body" said the figure

"I'm not going to let you do that easily." said David

"Hahahahhaha, but in the case of right now. I don't think you frankly have a choice here."

David made another attempt to move. However, he was still frozen in the air. Even if he was able to move, he wouldn't be able to do anything.

As the Made In Heaven bloodline had immense power, and was thought to be god like beings. Having powers that can devour planets. However, legend has it, the bloodline was destroyed as they themselves had a civil war. Seemingly destroying all of the bloodline. Nevertheless, it seems like there are remaining Made In Heaven members.

"You shall have no worry, I will do all the work." said the figure.

"Don't touch me!" responded David

"Hmmm. Why? This will grant you unlimited god-like powers. And eventually you can become one with god. Plus I don't think you even have a choice." continued the figure.

Suddenly, the figure started to deform. Eventually becoming a crystal. The crystal dives straight into David's stomach. David felt immense power burning through his veins. David could feel his body burning up. He felt like all his energy was burned out at once. However he could have another source of energy inside of him. Seemingly feeling another being inside his body.

With a massive amount of power that did not belong to him inside of him. He felt strange. He was tired as all of his own energy was seemingly burnt out, however the energy from another kept him up. Once the entirety of the crystal emerged into him, David fainted.

Suddenly, David was teleported back to his room in the spaceship. With him laying in a weird position, it was a big struggle for David to stand up. David was still unsure if the interaction with the legendary being was real. However, he was definitely sure that he underwent something. As his energy was entirely burnt out. And he could feel seemingly another being inside of his consciousness and body. However as of right now, the being was too weak and young to do anything. David could feel there was a large amount of energy and life force that was not his being inside of him.

Without much energy, David was forced to go in a resting state. It would take a long time for him to recover from the strange incident.

# CHAPTER 18

Heavily geared men, busted through the entrance of the safehouse. On the shoulder of the armor of the armed men, it was a rose with a bullet on it. Gordom remembered that this logo was the RoseLaFire. Gordom quickly took cover, remembering that they were here to capture people like him.

Suddenly, the room was bombed with a flash grenade. Momentarily blinding Gordom, which was an opportunity for the armed men to capture him. Gordom stayed silent, thinking that the armed men had not discovered him yet. Seconds later Gordom's vision had been restored. A clattering sound was next to Gordom. Gordom looked to the left.

A grenade rolled next to him. It was deemed to explode in a second. By the time Gordom was able to realize it, it was already too late.

The grenade exploded.

The grenade destroyed the room he was staying in. Also blasting Gordom out of the destroyed building.

Gordom lost consciousness and was sure he would not survive.

It had seemed like hours had passed. Gordom had regained consciousness. Gordom felt warmth and comfort. He opened his eyes, where he was met by the darkness of night. He felt the warmth of the icy night, and the comfort of the unsettling darkness. The night sky being the blanket of the night, and the snow being the berth of his mind.

Gordom sat up expecting himself to be in the wilderness all alone. However, he was wrong. He seemed to be in a campsite. With an open fire burning by the feets near him. With seemingly no one being near him, Gordom was quite confused as he was unsure of who put him under refuge.

Despite the confusing situation, Gordom walked around assuming that someone else was around.

He was in the deepness of the woods, Gordom was surrounded by trees in all directions. His campsite was only in a small opening in the forest. However, Gordom was able to catch the slimmest source of light in the distance. The first thought was to encounter the light source. However after a quick consideration, Gordom decided not to directly encounter the light source. As the holder of the light source is unknown. It could be an enemy or an ally. However, there was no way to know that. Gordom decided to carefully approach the light source, hoping that it would do no harm. If it's an enemy, slowly retract back to the campsite.

Gordom slowly sneaked toward the light source. Gordom had to be scrupulous since the uneven terrain had twigs that could send him to the blue. With Gordom being extremely careful, taking each step very carefully. He moved at a very slow pace, he noticed that the light source was also moving. Moving at a much faster pace, in the same direction as Gordom. Gordom had to speed things up, as he would not be able to catch up without at least going twice the speed as his speed now. Gordom started jogging, at first still taking precaution, however he would have to run to catch up.

So that's what Gordom did, he ran full speed toward the light source, hoping he would be able to catch up quickly. Without much precaution, Gordom was exposed to danger. However, that did not go through Gordom's head. He did not think of the consequences at the moment. However things would go very wrong.

Gordom got insanely close to the light source, however when he peeked to see who or what it was, he stepped on a twig. The sound was low however it was loud enough to be heard.

Instantaneously, the light source disappeared. It was very strange how quick the light source went out. At first, Gordom did not think much of this. He decided to turn back and go back to the campsite. However, something felt eerie, it was unnatural how fast the light source disappeared.

Gordom unintentionally turned back, planning to return to the mysterious campsite. Expecting to see nothing but the forest. He was dead wrong.

Gordom felt extreme coldness behind him. The feeling of dread verklempt his body. He could perceive a scent of cruelty. His blood suddenly became direly cold. Thoughts of the enjoyment of murder and mass slaughtering suddenly emerged from his mind. Images of sluaghtering and murder flashed before his own mind and eyes. Disturbing thoughts and images entered Gordom's mind, however he did not know where it came from. And frankly he could not stop it.

However, something made Gordom think it was ok to enjoy these shameful and agitating thoughts. Gordom was deeply distrubed and disgusted, however he could not do anything.

"Don't look back... hehehe" said a creepy voice.

Suddenly, Gordom was forced to turn his head around. As much as Gordom wanted to resist, he could not. An unnatural force was making him turn around. Moments later, Gordom was able to confront whoever or whatever it was.

However, when he was forced to turn around, he was met by a scene instead of a face. A bright light gazed into Gordom's unprotected eye. There was a circle of armed men, all with weapons with mass destruction. All held into the center of the surrounding area. Gordom wondered what or who was at the gunpoint.

Suddenly, he was able to move around again. Abruptly, Gordom heard a familiar

voice.

"Please don't, we are innocent." cried a voice

A voice he hadn't heard in months and months. Frankly he could not identify who the voice was from instantly. Quickly, he remembered this high pitched and warm voice.

It was his older sisters, with much shock. Gordom ran straight for the circle, seeing what he was not supposed to see. His entire family being tied by metal chains onto the ground. His older sister, his mother, and his younger brother were all tied to the ground seemingly accepting the punishment.

"Listen, it's not because you committed the crime that we made up to have a reason to kill you." said one of the armed men.

"It's because of your son. Yeah the one that you all thought died. Ohhhh no, he is alive and well. He is an enemy of ours, he gained supernatural powers that can possibly go against us." continued the armed men.

Suddenly, Gordom was filled with anger. He jumped inside of the circle, hoping that if they let his family go, he was captured. However, no one seemed to see him. He seemed to be invisible to the world he was in.

"I'm here, let them go!"Gordom screamed his life out.

However, not a single soul heard him. Moments later, shots were fired. The bullets went straight through Gordom's chest, hitting and killing his family.

The moment had suddenly slowed down. At that moment, the bullet had not hit yet. Gordom had to slowly watch his family being slaughtered. The pain and hatred was multiplied through this moment. The closer the bullet got to his family, the more pain he went through. It had seemed like an emotional bullet had burst through his heart. The pain in his heart was unexplainable, the slowness of the moment made him suffer more. It felt like how dripping water can penetrate stone through thousands and thousands of years. But it was sped up by millions and millions of times. But it had a rain of emotions. But it was all live flesh. But it was fresh that Gordom had been with and loved for more than a decade.

When the bullet was about to hit, the scene suddenly stopped. Everything had freezed. Moments later, everything around him dissolved into millions of particles. Out of the blue, a clear image of the murdering occurred inside of his brain. Making him remember that clear and fresh picture.

Seconds later, Gordom began to fall down the spiral of nothingness. At this point, Gordom lost his mind. Constantly remained of the clear murdering of his family. He fell through the floors of his dignity. Free falling into the ocean of regret and pain. Entering the dimension of wintercearig, and opening the door to hiraeth.

Moments passed, Gordom just seemingly kept free falling into the nothingness. Suddenly, something was on the bottom. He could not tell what was at the bottom, as Gordom was still extremely high up in the air. Moments later, Gordom was able to see the ground. The surroundings had highly guarded buildings, with each building being extremely large. The buildings are being fenced in by breathtaking lasers. And guard towers that can erase anything from existence in a 800 mile radius.

With Gordom seemingly falling into the main building of the highly secured base. Again, no one seemed to see Gordom. With the guard tower having the ability to blast Gordom. And being easily spotted, not a single soul seemed to notice Gordom. Seconds later, Gordom's body fazed through the building. Falling through the building, Gordom could tell it was some kind of laboratory. Everything in the building was black. However, it seemed like the blackness gave out its own light. The whole building gave off an uncomfortable vibe. It had seemed like inhumane things had been done in this very room. Gordom saw something familiar down below on the first floor. With each second getting closer, Gordom was able to see who it was. Gordom landed on the second floor in the building. Being able to see the whole first floor.

Gordom saw himself, Scarlet, and another figure he did not know, in the building. Without much understanding of what is happening, he was sure this didn't happen yet. It must be fake or from the future.

The figure he did not know had a distinct feature. The right arm of the hoster had a weird arm. The arm was distinctly different from the rest of the body. The arm was blood red, with seemingly sharp claws. The arm had similar features to a bird, it had feathers on the under forearm. And a phoenix shaped feature on the above forearm. The hoster of the arm had a blazing red attire. With a flame red leather jacket, and maroon jeans, the hoster had a stunning cluster of blonde hair. The hoster had just a little bit of red on his hair. The hoster was about six feet one with a glazing pair of shining red iris.

Suddenly, the entrance into the building was shut. The figures began to search around the building. They were seemingly searching for something. Even though they had nowhere to exit. They did not show a scent of being worried. Suddenly, the figure with the weird arm, lit up a small source of fire on his finger. Even though the source of the fire was small, it was able to light up the entire first floor. Moments later, one of the walls opened up. Inside being a three headed lion ravenously roaring. Multiple beams of metal, stopped the lion from leaving the opened area. All of the figures looked to the right where the three headed lion was located. Seconds later, the beams of metal were dropped. Letting the beast free, it went straight for Scarlet. As she was the least physically capable. Scarlet released sparks of gold dust, seemingly wanting to calm the beast down without harming the beast. However, mental manipulation somehow did not work on the monster.

Then, the three headed lion leaped and was inches apart from harming Scarlet. Suddenly the moment seemed to slow down, the weird handed figure released a blast of gold flames seemingly wanting to burn the monster away from Scarlet. However, it was too slow. But, the Gordom down below, ran toward the monster and hurdled into a position where he was able to kick away the monster before hurting Scarlet. However, the current Gordom was confused. As it was impossible for one to run about 25 feet that fast, and be able to do it in the matter of milliseconds. And the fact that, Gordom's kick alone was able to send the monster flying.

"Watchout!" yelled the weird armed figured

He was warning them of the fire blast, the gold flames were inches away from burning them. Suddenly, Gordom was able to teleport from the spot to in the middle of the air with Scarlet in his arms.

"Ahhhh, my bad guys, bad timing." said the weird armed figure

"You're fine Maxentius, next time we just gotta be more careful." said Gordom

By the time he finished the sentence, he was able to safely land on the ground. Scarlet was also able to land on the ground with virtually no damage. However, something seemed wrong with her. Her face became pure pink, she seemed distracted by something. However, there was no time to ask her why. The reason being that the room was slowly getting filled with water.

Suddenly, the beast was able to stand on its feet again. However, the beast seemed to have something in its mind. It jumped and threw its paws at Gordom. Gordom guarded but he was knocked back. However, the three headed lion kept attacking Gordom. The continuous attack surprised Gordom tremendously. The three headed lion attacked a lot more aggressively than before. It seemed like something happened that alarmed the monster. Even though the hits were hard, the monster dropped its ease, making it vulnerable to other attacks.

Maxentius, the figure with the weird arm, from the center of his strange hand, blasted out a beam of blood red fire. It took form in a phoenix, made a flying motion, and directly hit the three headed lion. Knocked it far from Gordom, who somehow was not harmed at all.

The three headed lion roared in pain, its body was badly burnt. Somehow, the fire kept burning, even though a foot of the ground was filled up with the on going water. The fire kept burning even underwater.

"The more the monster screams, the hotter the fire will be," said Maxentius.

"Put it out of its misery already," said Scarlet.

"Alright, fine." responded Maxentius.

With a final blast of fire, the monster was dead. However, something that worried them more was the rising water. They would have to find an opening for them to evacuate either out of the building or going up a level. Suddenly, a small opening on the ceiling of the room opened up. The first thought was to quickly go up the opening. However, Gordom had another thought.

"Since, the water is not that deep, we should find more spots to evaluate, in case something happens." suggested Gordom calmly.

"Good idea, but hurry because very soon the room will be filled with water," said Scarlet.

Gordom tried to go back from where they entered, however again the door was shut. Gordom tired to use brute force to force is open. However, once he made heavy contact with the door. He was knocked into the air.

"Woah, this door reflected my attack." said Gordom surprisingly.

Moments later, the water got to their waist. Though another opening was not found, they had to leave the first floor. Gordom held Scarlet by the hands and somehow was able to boost himself and Scarlet into the opening. As for Maxentius, he formed a pair of glowing red bird wings from his back. The wings carelessly flapped up its way up to the second floor. Once everyone safely evaluated to the second floor, the real Gordom was lifted up from the first floor to the second by an unknown force. The real Gordom landed on the corner of the second floor. Even though everyone was able to escape the first floor, the water was still rising. Rising faster than ever before.

Gordom had tried to close the opening, however, it was impossible. The material of the opening was seemingly able to deflect any attack or brute force.

Suddenly, another part of the wall was opened, and released another monster. This time it was a large anaconda with sharp metal objects as its scales. Suddenly, it charged at seemingly everyone as of its massive size. Though the monster was colossal in size, it moved at incredible speed for its size.

"Ahhhhhhhhhhh!" screamed Maxentius in a barbarous way.

Maxentius raised his arm, and blasted a small source of bright red fire. However, seconds later, the small source of fire became a sea of fire. Hoping the sea of fire would crush the anaconda by the extreme heat. Seconds passed, everyone froze hoping that the anaconda would be dead. Moments, no sudden movement from the anaconda. Gordom thought the Anaconda was dead, as he stepped forward to check. Once his foot landed, the anaconda shot itself forward toward Gordom. However, Gordom was able to react fast enough. He blocked both of his hands. However, it was able to pierce through Gordom's skin. He was knocked down towards the wall and knocked out unconscious. Before the mutated Anaconda could continue to attack the unconscious Gordom, Scarlet stepped in. This time her mind powers worked on the monster. She was able to temporarily freeze the monster. By the short opening, she was able to do something strange. An unexpected yet powerful ability.

Using the short time, she was able to learn everything about the monster. Understanding its powers and its weaknesses, she had a natural upper hand against the beast. Adding on to her overwhelming ability of mind manipulation. After she understood the weaknesses of the creature, she began her plan.

Once the time freeze broke, she carried Gordom on her arm and stood in a defensive stance. Suddenly, Maxentius jumped upwards toward the upper ceiling and threw some smoke bombs which distracted the monster, leaving Scarlet open for an open attack. She jumped and got a direct hit on the bottom of the monster's jaw. Somehow launching the monster upwards. Maxentius suddenly appeared before Scarlet and launched several fire balls toward the monster. The monster was knocked back several feet. Not moving an inch, the monster was defeated.

After the victory, Scarlet put down the unconscious Gordom and started to seemingly diagnose him. She gave a fretful look toward Gordom.

Booom! The ground shook forcefully, a great force of wind blew in their direction. When they looked in that direction, everyone was surprised.

Somehow the anaconda was still alive, with its metal blade scales. It was about to attack, not alerted of its being. The anaconda was seconds away from striking and would have killed Scarlet.

When Scarlet looked to the left, there was Gordom blocking the attack with his left arm. This time the sharp blades were not able to pierce through his skin. Suddenly, Gordom got a hold of the anaconda with his hands. Gripping the sharp blades with his bare hands, upper cutting the monster's lower chin with his knee.

The monster was knocked in the air for several seconds. Gordom somehow jumped on air, getting to the monster in the matter of milliseconds. While in the air, Gordom kept hitting the sharp blades on the anaconda's body with his bare fist. He was insanely fast, seemingly being able to teleport. Attacking the anaconda all over the monster's body. However, the attacks as far as anyone can tell was doing nothing. There was no evidence of blood or any damage.

However, for some reason, Scarlet was smirking. Gordom was losing energy, his movements became slower and the attacks became softer. Finally, Gordom gave the anaconda a heavy hit on the stomach for the final time. Both Gordom and the anaconda landed on the ground.

When Gordom landed back on the ground, his hand was covered with blood. However, the blood was not his. It was perhaps something else's blood. Suddenly, blood starts leaking from the anaconda. The blood leaked from the creaks of the blade scales. The sharp blades were actually a suit of armor that naturally grew, but the sharp blades penetrated the anaconda's actual scales and killed the anaconda.

"Good job, you seemed to know the metal blades are not the actual scales." said a random voice.

Suddenly, a big screen was shown from a part of the wall that retracted into itself.

"Hello, Gordom, Scarlet, Maxentius" continued the voice.

"Welcome to my palace, isn't it beautiful?" said the voice

"How on Earth do you think this is a beautiful Morrigan! And we are gonna take that box" shouted Gordom

"Ohhh, are you talking about my box of all beings?" responded the Morrigan

"Ha, you came up with the name for that damn box. More like the box of all dread and harm!" said Gordom.

"Haha, no matter what you call it. You are not stopping me from achieving world peace." responded Morrigan.

"What? How dare you call that peace? You are basically burying people alive. How is that peace?" cried Gordom.

"First of all, I am helping the world by killing the evil. However, I am accidentally hurting people." responded Morrigan

"You are purposefully killing the people for your own good." responded Gordom.

"I am helping the universe, but I also get an award. A hero must get what a hero deserves. So I am rewarded that I can become one with the death gods." responded Morrigan.

"Listen, I don't care about what you get. We are gonna take that box from you before you can do more harm." said Gordom.

"Well, I'd like to see you try." responded Morrigan in an arrogant manner.

Suddenly, the ceiling opened up, revealing the seemingly final boss. The 12 feet figure slowly landed on the ground. The figure made the real Gordom feel cold and dreadful. It seems like every vein in Gordom's had been killed.

"If you want the box, you can have it. But you have to defeat me first." said Morrigan.

"Hmmm, you have no idea what is about to hit you." said Maxentius.

"Ohhh, Maxentius I haven't seen you in a while." said Morrigan.

"Yeah, since you killed my whole village," said Maxentius.

"I do remember that, but I mean you wouldn't be who you are today without that event." responded Morrigan.

"I swear to god Morrigan, I will kill you," said Maxentius.

"Calm down, we don't need to kill her, we just need the box." said Scarlet.

"Ohhh Scarlet of the Mind Manipulation, it's an honor to meet you. If you ever change your mind, feel free to join me." said Morrigan.

"Anyways, do you guys want the box, or shall I keep it?" continued Morrigan.

Suddenly, Gordom struck from behind. However the attempt was deflected easily by Morrigan.

"Gordom of the Undying, very impatient." said Morrigan in a disappointed tone as Gordom was deflect back.

"Well, I guess let us begin." continued Morrigan.

Suddenly, Maxentius sprayed a colossal amount of gold dust on Morrigan out of his strange hand. Morrigan formed a circle shield out of seemingly dark matter. Confining herself inside the shield of dark matter. Suddenly, Maxentius grasped his hand and inside of the dark matter shield was a series of explosions. The explosions let out seemingly hundreds of explosions in the span of 10 seconds. Moments later, the dark matter shield opened up. A large amount of smoke came out of the opening. When the dark matter shield began to crumble, nothing was inside of the shield.

"Hmmmm, your little tricks can't trick me. But it seems like you have grown from our last encounter. But it's still not enough" said Morrigan, who suddenly appeared from behind Maxentius.

Morrigan appeared to have copied Maxentius' ability. She suddenly blasted the explosions back at Maxentius. Gordom suddenly appeared in front of Maxentius, shielding Maxentius.

"Hmmm Gordom, it seems like you can dance with me for some time." said Morrigan

"Don't underestimate me!" said Gordom.

"Shall we begin?" said Morrigan

Suddenly, Morrigan leaned and quickly floated towards Gordom. Gordom made a series of hand signs and ran towards Morrigan.

Suddenly, the situation became blurry. The real Gordom experienced a time glitch. Suddenly, the situation changed, with Gordom lying on the ground seemingly defeated. Scarlet in the middle of the room with her skin smokingly red. Everything seemed to doesn't make sense. Suddenly the room started to crumble, seemingly a portal had been opened. A portal to space has been opened in the middle of the room. The portal started to eat away the room and seemed to devour the whole room. With the room being deleted at an alarming rate.

With the portal making unusual sounds, everyone's voice was over-lapped by the loud sound. Suddenly, the real Gordom's perspective was shifted into one with the other Gordom. With the portal slowly sucking Gordom into the unknown space.

"No, don't do it, it's not worth it." shouted the other Gordom.

"I'm sorry Gordom, but I believe it's time for me to go." responded Scarlet.

Gordom stood up making his way towards Scarlet. The portal was devouring the building and sucking whoever or whatever into it. With much force, Gordom had to use incredible force to get to the center of the room where Scarlet was.

A few feet in front Scarlet was a collapsed Morrigan, however she was still conscious. Moments later, Gordom was able to get to Scarlet.

"I'm sorry but it has to be done." said Scarlet

"No I'm sure...." said Gordom who was interrupted by Scarlet.

Scarlet dived into Gordom. Scarlet hugged Gordom, interrupting him.

"I'll look after you in Heaven." said Scarlet.

Gordom froze in space in disbelief, speechless. The room was half devoured already. It was clear that was the only solution. Suddenly, Scarlet gave Gordom a little shove. Slowly falling into the unknown space.

Scarlet sent a dust of magic towards Gordom. Before the magic could hit, Scarlet mouthed something. Something Gordom hadn't heard in years. *I love you...*

The magic made Gordom forget everything. Suddenly, Scarlet became blazing red. Then Gordom fainted, not knowing what happened in the end.

# CHAPTER 19

Bump, Bump, Bump, Bump. David woke in a cold sweat, his heart beating heavily. His body felt heavy, just like his heartbeat. He felt extreme heat coming out of his tired out body. However he also had extreme coldness blowing into his body. It felt like he was in the center of the fire and ice. It felt like torture but he had no idea what was torturing him.

David felt extremely tired, however another source of energy was keeping him up in this torturous condition. David used the remaining of his energy to get on the bed as he had just collapsed on the floor. As soon David made it to his bed, he collapsed immediately.

"Oiiii, get up, get up." said a familiar voice.

David looked across the room. There was no one there talking to him. David thought he was imagining a voice. But no, the voice kept calling for him.

"Get up, get up. Your body is hungry. You know I grant you powers, but I gotta survive too." said the voice.

"Who is talking?" questioned David.

"Me, ohh wait I haven't introduced myself yet. I am the Made In Heaven figure that chose you as my new body." said the voice

"Can you just get out of my body please." responded David.

"In your dreams, I gotta reincarnate through your body. In return I give out god-like powers." responded the voice.

"Anyways, get up. Your body gotta eat." continued the voice.

"I frankly don't have the energy to speak. How am I supposed to get up and walk to get food?" responded David.

"Fine, I'll grant you energy. But be careful because you will have a tremendous power boost." said the voice.

"Huh, wait what?" said David.

"Too late!" responded the voice.

Suddenly, David shot right out of his bed. David stepped down from his bed. Somehow feeling full of energy. Suddenly, his movement became significantly faster. He felt strength and power.

"Now, hurry up before you collapse again, it's only for a limited time." said the voice.

David quickly exited his room hoping he would figure this situation out.

"You know what you're thinking about right?" said the voice.

"Huh?" said David.

"Yes you heard me, I know what you are thinking about." the voice. Anyways, go get some food. You're hungry." said the voice.

"I think I know my body more than you." said David.

David stumbled out of his room. Some reason, it was a lot harder to control his own body. This body felt powerful and seemed like he had a lot less control over it.

"Why can't I walk regularly?" asked David

"Oh I don't know, maybe because you just get a massive amount of energy and power from a god-like figure." responded the voice in a proud manner.

"Umm ok, then I'm definitely gonna break something," said David.

"I really don't care, just get food," said the voice.

David walked how he used to walk. However, suddenly the pacing became incredibly fast. David could not slow down, the speed just became faster and faster. Somehow, his body is able to keep up with the speed. Moments later, they were at the end of the hallway. There was no way David was stopping without crashing into the wall.

"Stop running," said the voice.

"I can't, I can't control the power you gave me." responded David.

"Stupid Mortals, just stop." responded the voice.

"I can't, I don't even know how my body is keeping up." said David.

"Just stop running, is it that hard?"

"Oh my god, are you gonna just complain and not help me."

"How, it's your body."

"It's the power that you gave me."

"Mortals complain about everything."

"Says you! Tell me how to stop running."

"I don't know, usually I run way faster than this. And I just stop."

"Of course you will run a lot faster, you are a god."

"Ha, yes you understand my mighty powers."

"Just help me stop running."

"Fine, I'll take away the pow...."

BANG! David penetrated through the graphene wall. The immense speed and force sent him flying into another room. Even though the immense force penetrated him through graphene. Though it penetrated a wall of the strongest material in the world, David felt close to nothing. David crashed into the cafeteria.

"Sorry, I ran a little bit too fast." apologies David.

After David got up, he went to get some food. After David got some food, he returned to his room to eat.

"That did not hurt at all." said David

"Yea, maybe because I granted your god-like power?" suggested the voice.

"What am I supposed to say, thank you?" said David

"Yes, because you are so fortunate that I chose you as my vessel." responded the voice.

"When did I want to become your vessel again?" asked David.

"Ok, please just eat the food." responded the voice.

"Ok now you're begging me to do something."

"It's for the good of all of us. If you die, I'll die too. That is why I am offering power. So that you don't die."

"So what's our relationship here?"

"You are my vessel, I am you in the future. You're gonna be dead once I become fully evolved in your body. But I want you to live long enough to make it to that point."

"So you want me to live just to die later."

"If you want to put it that way, yes."

"So why should I not end your plans right here, right now?"

"I mean do you really want to do that? You are young, full of potential and you will be doing great things. I can see your future."

"Ummm, so will I become you?"

"Oh, you definitely don't have to worry about that. I will make sure it's successful. Thank you for worrying."

"What do you mean by you'll make sure?"

"Oh I can't see that part of the future, I can't see my future. So if I can't have your future and mine at that period of time, that means I will take over your body."

"Ohhh lord."

"But I'm not particularly sure what really happens. Maybe the unthinkable might happen."

"What do you mean by the unthinkable?"

"Oh don't worry it has only occurred like once in millions of years."

"Well what is it?"

"It's basically when the vessel and the owner kind of become friends and they merge together, living in the same body."

"So the vessel won't have to die?"

"Yea basically. Don't think I will do that, I hate mortals."

"Yea not particularly good for me."

"Anyways, go eat whatever you have here."

"You mean bacon and eggs?"

"Yea whatever that's called."

"You never had bacon and eggs?"

"No, why would I? I live in the heavens, why would I eat such lower level food? We eat legendary fruits that only grow once a billion years."

"Cool I guess?"

"Anyways let me taste whatever you have there."

Moments later, David finished the bacon and eggs.

"Damn! That was delicious! Woah we don't have that in Heaven" said the voice.

"Who is talking now?" responded David

"Ok, I was wrong, not everything in the mortal world is bad," said the voice.

"Thank you, by the way, what does the legendary fruit taste like?" responded David.

"It tastes like that fruit that's red inside but black and green inside."

"Watermelon?"

"Yeah watermelon, but with just a little bit of a taste of like lead and metal."

"Um, that's disgusting."

"Well, it was the only thing there and it gave you power."

"So will your powers go away if you don't eat the fruit?"

"Oh, that was more than one million years ago. It's my bloodline that gives me powers."

"So what is the fruit for?"

"Well it's basically for pressure, we don't really need food but we eat for pleasure. And plus I've eaten since most of my bloodline was destroyed, which was almost five hundred years ago."

"Oh wow you have existed for that long?"

"I've been alive for almost 15 million years."

"And how many vessels have you had?"

"Only about 3, because every 5 million, I need a new body."

"And nobody has given you a name?"

"Well no, since I don't talk to all of my vessels."

"What do you call each other among your bloodline?"

"Well, I have a name, it's just not in your language."

"I'm gonna give you a name, I don't know how to call you."

"Go on!"

"How about Hoseki? It means gem in Japanese and your body was made out of gems."

"You know not bad, the first time I've agreed with a mortal."

"It seems like you were a brat when you were still alive."

"Wow, I am offended by your rude words. But I was a little aggressive and inconsiderate but that's not the point."

"Anyhow have we decided that Hoseki is now your name from now on?"

"Sure, seems good to me."

"By the way, I was wondering where you live in my body?"

"If you reveal your stomach, you will see a special pattern. In which is a curse mark that I placed on you. I am in the curse mark."

David flipped a part of his shirt open, and there it was. A triangular shape with a large X in the center appeared on David's stomach.

"Ohhh so you live here."

"Well, I don't live in it. It's a curse that helps you transform into me. But I basically live in your consciousness."

"Umm that's weird."

"But you can actually see me and interact with me in your consciousness. But you'll have to find the way."

"Well frankly, I don't want to meet you."

"I am gonna take away the power that I gave you; since you just ate."

"To talk about the powers aga..."

Suddenly, David felt extremely weak. It felt like the power was suddenly sucked out of him. David collapsed onto the ground. He had a sudden dizziness. His became extremely blurry. Moments later, David seemed to recover from whatever just had happened.

"What was that?" asked David

"A price you have to pay." responded Hoseki

"Well, what's the price?" asked David.

"It's a side effect from the large amount of energy extraction."

"I am guessing I have to endure that everytime I borrow energy from you."

"Yes you do, unless we merge, then that won't happen."

"How do I do that?"

"Well, there are two types of merging. One is me taking over your body, the other is we both exist in your body."

"So how does the second one work, so we have to sign basically a contract. Once I basically agree, you will have the power to undo the curses on your stomach."

"So would you please just agree?"

"No, I'd rather have this body myself than sharing. And since it's still your body, you will have much more power over it than me."

"If you don't, I will end your plans right now."

"Well, I won't let that happen, because I will give you an immense amount of energy so that you won't die."

"Our relationship here is very interesting."

"Indeed, though I am sure somethings will change"

"Anyways, I got something I need to check out."

Then Hoseki went silent, David now using his own energy. He exited his room seemingly wanting to see something. Once David exited the room, he was met by Tony Musk.

"Hello David, how are you doing?" asked Tony Musk.

"Oh I'm doing quite well actually, I took a rest and nothing has really happened." responded David.

"That's good to hear, where are you doing?" questioned Tony Musk

"I was actually about to check out the kid that we saved from a while ago." answered David.

"Oh ok do you know where he is? He is in the 5th guest bedroom." said Tony Musk

"Ok, thanks I'll be back after I talk to him." suggested David.

David quickly exited the area, going to the opposite side of the spaceship.

"Who was that?" asked Hoseki

"Tony Musk, the guy that's helping me to become stronger and find a friend." responded David.

"That guy gives me weird vibes. It feels like he is hiding something." said Hoseki

"Really, he seems like a good guy." suggested David.

"Trust me, I've met more people than you. He doesn't seem truthful. I don't know, he seems complicated." said Hoseki.

"Umm, Ok? I don't get what you're trying to say." said David.

"I'm just saying, he might be your downfall. You shouldn't trust that man." suggested Hoseki.

"Anyways, keep quiet, I have to talk to someone." responded David.

David quickly hustled to the opposite side of the spaceship. With an intention of some kind, Tony Musk suddenly ran to the left of the main area. It had seemed like Tony Musk did not know that David was there. David stayed in the hidden, remaining in place he was able to get a clear view of the area.

Suddenly, Tony Musk placed his hands on one of the walls. And the wall was retracted into the ground, revealing another wall. He placed his hand on the wall revealing a passcode of some kind. Tony Musk quickly typed in the password and in a flash he disappeared.

Though David was not about to see where Tony Musk was, he was sure that Tony Musk was hiding something. With much in mind, David kept everything to himself.

"See, I told you he was suspicious. You shouldn't trust him." said Hoseki.

"Now I know what you're talking about. He has been suspicious recently. Because I've suspected him for some time now." said David.

"We should keep this by ourselves. Just to be safe." said Hoseki

"I agree, we need more information." responded David.

David was desperate to see what was on that wall. However, he knew he could, since there were dozens of hidden cameras in this one room.

David walked naturally across the room, seemingly resumed to his original goal of meeting someone. Moments later, he arrived at the guest room.

*Knock, Knock.* David knocked on the door two times.

"Yes...." said a deep croaked voice.

The voice was unbelievable, as the person David was talking to was a child. There was no possible way the child could have that deep of a voice. A heavy breathing sound could be heard behind David. Coldness wrapped David's body. David looked back, meeting a pitch black figure. The figure seemingly did not have a body shape. However the face of the figure could be clearly seen.

It was a tall and majestic figure, it had seemed like the face of the figure was burned badly. However, it did not seem like it was natural. As the entire face was pitch black, and the eyes were blood red.

"Ahhhh the smell of humans. Delicious." said the figure.

"Oh no David, I suggest you run," said Hoseki.

The figure swung its arm at David. Hitting David and sending him flying across the hallway. The figure suddenly teleported in front of David. Started continuously hitting David. The attacks were extremely fast, and it felt heavy. Every shot David took, it had seemed like more energy was cut from his body.

After a countless amount of attacks, it had seemed like the creature was going for the last attack. As the creature slowed down, it had seemed like the last attack would knock David out.

As the fist of the figure got closer and closer, David's consciousness seemed to fade.

# CHAPTER 20

Suddenly, Gordom shot up in cold sweat, ending up back at the campsite. The warmth of the fire made Gordom feel at home.

"You have finally woken up," said a familiar voice.

"Where am I? What happened?" said Gordom.

"The enemies attacked our secret camp, we counter and they are gone now. Fortunately no deaths have been found yet." said the familiar voice

"Wait what?" said Gordom as he struggled to open his eyes.

"I found you in the riverbed of the jungle." answered the familiar voice

Gordom was hardly able to open his eyes.

"Scarlet is that you?" asked Gordom.

"Yes it is." said the familiar voice.

"Wait so what happened?" asked Gordom.

"So we were attacked by the RoseLaFire, but we were able to counter them. However, there was an explosion that destroyed the building. And you were right next to the explosion that sent you out on to a river that led you here. And when I was searching for survivors, I found you unconscious. And for some reason I found you again in the middle of the jungle, where a nightmaremaker was near you." said Scarlet.

"So what happened to the camp?" asked Gordom

"Well, We are planning to relocate to a better spot." answered Scarlet in a calm voice.

"Where are the others?" asked Gordom

"A lot of people are missing, we are still not sure where to meet up, but the current plan is to set up small temporary camps." answered Scarlet.

"Can I help you find some of the missing people?" asked Gordom.

"Sure, but right now you will need to rest. Since the Nightmaremaker has done some colossal damage to your mental state." said Scarlet.

"What is that?"

"It's nothing, I have already deleted most of the fake memories the monster has placed in you."

"What memories?"

"It's very complicated, don't worry about it. You need rest."

The next day, Gordom had a lot more energy. Even though much of his energy was restored, there was not much memory of what had happened to him. Though Scarlet had said she erased much of the memory, he could still have a vague image of the seemingly erased memory. He remembered a flash of bright colors and a strange scene of unknown figures.

"Are you up Gordom?" asked Scarlet

"Yea, I just woke up." responded Gordom.

"Hurry up and get ready, we have to go find the missing ones." said Scarlet.

"Oh ok, is there a river I can clean myself a bit?"

"Yes, 1 minute to the south."

"Be back in a few minutes."

Gordom started heading south of the woods. The sound of pouring water became louder and louder. Suddenly, bright light flashed on the corner of Gordom's eye. Something was on the ground waiting to be discovered. Gordom quickly turned to see what was flashing. On the ground, there he found an unusual piece of object. A green pearl necklace that someone must have lost.

Gordom searched the area for the signs of the owner. However, no footsteps and not a single breath could be found near the necklace. Gordom decided to keep it and find the owner later. He continued to walk south as he was met by a river.

However, something felt eerie about this place. Someone has been to this place, a group of people. As the smell of gunpowder is undeniably heavy. Gordom slowly approached the river with much caution.

*Beep.* Flashes of red light lit up around Gordom. Revealing hidden gadgets that had been placed.

Suddenly, explosions setted off, splashing a huge wall of water around Gordom. Gordom fell on the group, as the huge amount of water hit him.

"AHA, I've got a gud one innit." said a voice.

Suddenly a human figure ran toward Gordom and jumped on Gordom.

"What are you doing?" shouted Gordom as he resisted the human figure.

"Oiii, wot are you doing here mate? Wot happened to ma fiesh?" said the human figure as he attempted to get off of Gordom.

"What do you mean fish, I am here to clean my face." responded Gordom in an irritated voice.

"No need to get mad here mate, I'm just here so I dont starve to deeth." said the figure

"Huh? You call that fishing? You are literally setting bombs." questioned Gordom.

"Well wot am I supposed to do, I'm smart and look young and that's all I do mate." responded the figure.

"How long have you been out here?" asked Gordom.

"Over a year mate, thiss is how I get foood mate." responded the figure.

"Ohh, um that's cool," said Gordom.

"By the way, my name is Erik. Erik Beasly. As I said before, I am smart and I don't look old." said Erik

"Ummm how old are you?" asked Gordom.

"I am 18, mate." responded Erik.

"That's not that old." suggested Gordom.

"I know mate, if I tell myself I keep telling myself that I won't look old, I will believe it someday. Wots ur name my good sir?" responded Erik.

"I'm Gordom, and I'm helping ProtectorTurquoise." said Gordom.

"Ohh, I've heard of them. I have wanted to join but I have no idea where to find them." said Erik.

"I'll bring you to my supervisor," said Gordom.

"Ok mate, thank you." said Erik.

Gordom and Erik quickly rushed back to camp, where they were met by an angry Scarlet.

"Gordom where have you been, it has been more than 25 minutes." questioned Scarlet.

"I'm sorry Scarlet, I met this fellow near the river." apologizes Gordom.

"Hello mate, yea I tried to blow him up because I thought he was a fiesh." said Erik.

"Um ok, but Gordom we have to go." said Scarlet.

"Wait a minute, Erik wants to join ProtectorTurquoise." said Gordom.

"Yees mate, I am smart and I know how to build things like machines and bombs." proposed Erik.

"Um, so you want to work for us," said Scarlet.

"Yes, that's exactly wot I am saying." said Erik.

"You can come with us, we have somewhere to go," said Scarlet.

"Oh ok, thanks for giving me a chance mate." said Erik.

The group started moving towards the east. Suddenly, a mountainous amount of wind was thrown towards the group's being. Though the monstrous amount of wind blew into the group. Despite the difficulty, the group did not slow down. With the wind, was brought a wall of dust and sand. With litter scarps and debrises of metal, the wall was destined to hit the group.

Scarlet raised both of her hands attempting to do something. However, before Scarlet was able to do anything, Erik stepped multiple steps towards the sand wall.

"Het, get back here, that is very dangerous." shouted Scarlet.

"I will be fine." responded Erik in a confident manner.

Gordom and Scarlet looked at each other with visual confusion.

Suddenly, Erik pulled out a sphere-like object and held it in the palm of his hand. Moments later, the sphere started to ascend into mid air. A black dot appeared near the sphere. The black dot became larger and larger. And somehow was able to form a portal. The portal sucked all of the sand and the debris into this small sphere. Few seconds later, all of the sand

and the debris had been completely devoured by the sphere. Revealing an abandoned city which is filled with sand.

"Woah! Erik, how did you do that?" asked Gordom with Scarlet nodding.

"So basically I created a small vortex through this sphere mate and gathered all of the resources in the sand wall. In which I will use more inventions mate. And I call this Vulture" responded Erik in a proud tone.

"Wow, that is amazing! I did not know you knew how to make stuff like this. I am so sorry I underestimated your skills." said Scarlet.

"It's alright mate, I am glad you know now. But I have a lot more cool gadgets that I have made." responded Erik.

"Wait, where does the sand and the debris go?" asked Gordom.

"Right in here mate." said Erik as he held up another device of some kind.

The device was a cube made of unknown material. It had seemed like the cube was made out of smaller cubes.

"And what is that exactly?" questioned Gordom.

"It is a cube that gathers and organizes the resources I gathered from the Vulture. And as you can see the form of this can change, allowing flexible positions mate." responded Erik.

"Wait but how does this large amount of resources go into that small thing?" further questioned Gordom.

"It makes the resources very tiny and fits it into the small cubes that make up the whole cube. And if I want to access the material I can just call for the particular cube and take out the material I want mate. And I call this thing Collector." responded Erik.

"Wow, that is amazing. But we still have a long way to go, so we should hurry up." said Scarlet.

"Ohhh a long time, you didn't tell me that. I have us covered." said Erik as he toyed with the cube.

"What are you doing?" asked Scarlet.

"Trust me this is gonna speed up the journey. 1D please show." said Erik.

Suddenly, one cube became a bit bigger. Suddenly it revealed a small vehicle of some kind. Erik carefully carried the tiny vehicle with his fingers. He tossed the small vehicle onto the sand and waited for a few seconds.

"You guys back up a bit," said Erik.

Gordom and Scarlet backed up a few steps.

Suddenly, the vehicle became large. From a tiny object to a real vehicle.

"Hop on, don't we have a place to go to mate?" said Erik.

Scarlet and Gordom quickly go into the car. The car had a very strange appearance, with four large wheels supported by metal and a large spring. With also four smaller wheels on the top of the car both supported by metal and springs. Without a windshield they were all required to wear an eye protector and cloth face mask. The seats were also very strange. The seats seemed to be levitating in mid-air.

"Where are we going?" asked Erik.

"I have the coordinates. Do you want the coordinates?" responded Scarlet.

"Sure coordinates will work mate." responded Erik.

"Here are the coordinates. And it's on this planet only, not universal." said Scarlet as she seemingly implanted the coordinate into Erik's mind.

"Joseph open up coordinates please," said Erik.

"Ok Erik, coordinates are being pulled up." said a voice.

"Who was that?" questions Gordom.

"Ohhh my AI assistant Joseph, named after my uncle." responded Erik.

"Put in the coordinates from the keypad below," said Joseph.

Erik quickly entered the coordinates to the location. Moments later, the car started up.

"Going to Gardenth, Eter now. Estimated time is 120 minutes." said Joseph.

"Tie your seat belts and try not to stare because you will be extremely dizzy after this," said Erik.

"Umm Ok?" responded Gordom in a confused tone.

"But why th...." said Scarlet as she was cut off by the immense speed the car had suddenly brought up.

"This is the reason mate. And there will be a lot more huge bumps and leaps mate." answered Erik.

The car moved in incredible speed with it at least estimated going at 9000 miles per second. Despite the incredible speed, the car was pin drop silence. Somehow the car made no sound whatsoever. The car felt extremely lightweight, it felt that a man could lift up the car. Even though it felt lightweight, the car was extremely sturdy. With the car being able to drop from 5000 miles and not getting serious damages. Despite the difficult path the speed of the car has not decreased a single bit, and the rough road did not even scratch the body of the car.

"Woah, Erik, did you build this?" asked Gordom.

"Well not directly mate but yes I did build this," said Erik.

"How?" continued to question Gordom.

"I will explain later mate," said Erik.

Suddenly, the car started going up a hand hill. However, due to the lack of vision and the special seats there was no sign of going upwards for the passengers. Seconds after they reached the top, there was a deep drop. This time everyone saw the sudden change of terrain. Scarlet and Gordom were extremely worried about the deep drop. However, there was Erik sitting there unfazed by the drop.

Suddenly the car nose dived toward the sand, however the passengers were still facing straight and up front. The seats kept them from nose diving into the sand. And somehow the car was still stuck onto the sand, the car was basically driving vertically.

"What in the world is happening?" asked Gordom.

"Let me explain mate, so we have actual anti gravity seats that will stay in one position no matter what happens. And the wheels are stuck to the sand since the vehicle sends anti-vibration that makes all the sand near the area grasp onto the wheels therefore making it able to drive vertically. Mate it's as simple as that." responded Erik.

"And you did this all by yourself?" asked Scarlet.

"Well, I worked with some of my robots and machines I have made to make this. This is actually comparably simple if you matched them with my other inventions mate." responded Erik.

"I just still can't get past the thought that you built all of this by yourself," said Gordom.

"Yes I know, I worked my way up towards today. Which was both a painful and lovely experience mate." said Erik.

"Good for you. I think you would be very helpful in our organization." said Scarlet.

"Thank you mate. And also the car constantly searches the area for terrain changes and useful materials. By doing this I have basically mapped out everywhere I go mate." said Erik.

"Wow, that is incredible," said Gordom.

"But I am also considering adding flight and water transportation to this vehicle as well. The design is already complete but I don't have much materials on hand right now mate." said Erik.

"Ohh that is not a problem, we have tons of materials at the camp. Which we are going to right now." said Scarlet.

"Ohh that is great mate. I can probably finish the prototype by the end of the day." said Erik.

"How? Is it really that easy?" asked Gordom.

"I mean I have machines that help me mate, and the prototype model is already built on my computer. Which I can input into my building system which will finish the building by the end of the day mate." said Erik.

"Oh ok, is it possible to build more of these cars?" asked Scarlet.

"Of Course, I still have the model mate," said Erik.

"Ok, so can you make some cars for ProtectorTurquoise?" asked Scarlet.

"Yea sure, I just need enough materials." answered Erik.

"We have tons of materials at the camp," said Scarlet.

"But first I will make more of the Vulture and the Collector so gathering material and storing will be a lot easier. Therefore I can make a lot more things at the same time mate." said Erik.

"Sounds like a good plan to me." responded Scarlet.

Moments later, there seemed to be an obstacle stopping them to proceed. There was a large lake that stopped them from going to the other side. The first thought was to cross from the sides. However, the lake seemed to have no visible perimeter.

"What do we do here?" asked Gordom.

"Ohh we will be fine, trust me mate." said Erik.

Suddenly, the car dropped down doors and the interior of the car was covered by a foam like material. With the outer terrier also covered with a foam like material.

"Wait, I thought you hadn't added water transportation?" asked Gordom.

"Wait for it mate," said Erik.

The car drove right into the water. However, the car was still able to run. The car drove straight into the depth of the lake. However something seemed off. It had seemed like they were driving straight through the water. Instead of actually driving in water, the car was somehow pushing the water and creating a tunnel.

"So the car sends out sound waves which creates pressure and pushes away the water therefore creating a massive air bubble. And then the car can drive through the lake mate." said Erik.

"Are the sound waves what the foam is for?" asked Gordom.

"Yes it is mate, these are anti-vibration foam pads. Basically stopping the sound waves from entering the car and destroying our eardrums mate." said Erik

"At this point, I'm not even surprised nor moved at this point," said Gordom.

"And the air bubble moves with the car. So it's not a tunnel." said Erik.

"So the air pocket is not permanent?" asked Scarlet.

"Nope it is not permanent, it will move with the car and it will disappear when we reach land." said Erik.

"But you said you wanted to add water transportation to the vehicle. Is there something wrong with this?" asked Gordom.

"Well, it doesn't work when we are below 200 miles. Which is fairly shallow for the rarer resources to show up." said Erik.

"Ohh yea, I guess it is because the pressure down below is too much for the car to push away," said Scarlet.

"That is correct, the pressure below is too hard for the car to push off mate." said Erik.

Moments later, they were able to exit from the other side of the lake.

About an hour had passed, and the group had finally arrived at the campsite location. With the campsite being at the interference of a desert and a jungle.

"So this is the place you guys were talking about innit." said Erik.

"Good observation, normals wouldn't be able to see it." said Scarlet.

"Well, I don't see it. But I do sense something here, but mate, the structure is impressive." said Erik.

"Hmm, interesting." said Scarlet.

Suddenly, with a flick of a wrist. Scarlet sent out golden dust like materials forward. With the dust-like material disappearing instantly, a small room rose from the ground.

"Stay here for a bit," said Scarlet.

She walked toward the entrance of the room. With her hand, she was able to unlock the door into the room. Scarlet gave Erik and Gordom a hand sign to stay in place.

Scarlet carefully entered the room, the door was shut quickly. Suddenly, the walls became transparent. They reveal a room of a metal chair and a wooden table. The room seemed to be very hollow other than the two objects. The stillness in the room stuffed the area with heaviness and calmness.

There was Scarlet, arrogantly walking towards the chair. She placed her hand on the hair like how one would hold an infant.

With much care, he slowly dragged the scraping metal out and arrogantly sat.

As she gently placed both of her hands on the wooden table.

Suddenly the table opened up revealing a seemingly cup of tea in front of her.

With much calmness, Scarlet set her thin hands on the cup of tea.

Scarlet carefully sipped a mouthless tea and seemingly mouthed one word. Then she gently exited the room. And seemingly said one word.

"What was that?" asked Gordom.

"It was an identity test and a lie detector test," said Scarlet.

"Ahhh, I see. They wanted to see if you were the real you, but matching the motion of sipping tea. And they used a lie detector to tell if you're lying or being forced, innit mate." said Erik.

"Yes, that is completely correct." said Scarlet.

Seconds passed, a hole opened up from the ground, revealing a deep drop. The drop seemed to be endless. They could barely make out the borders of the hole as the hole was pitch blackness.

However, Scarlet jumped right into the deep hole.

"C'mon guys, hop in." said Scarlet as she fell into the deep hole.

Without much intricate direction, Gordom and Erik jumped into the hole. However, it had seemed like Erik knew what he was doing. As Erik dived head first into the hole. Gordom still showed a bit of concern for the bold action. Though he had several major concerns, seeing the others do it, he also jumped in.

"Umm Scarlet, what do we do here?" shouted Gordom.

"Don't do anything, just free fall, or if you want to nose dive into the hole." exclaimed Scarlet.

With still a lot of uncertainty, Gordom just let his body go. With more and more speed building up, there was a wave of wind blowing upwards. The large amount of contrast made it extremely difficult to go either way. As gravitation continued to suck him down the hole, the mass amount of wind continued to eject him upwards.

Gordom felt a strange energy inside of his stomach. It felt like his organs were twisting. It felt like there was a black hole twisting his organs away.

Through the pitch blackness, Gordom was able to see something strange. His entire torso disappeared. The bottom half of his body clung onto this small string that connected to the upper half of Gordom's body. Gordom attempted to touch the spiral vortex, however, before he could reach it. Gordom felt another powerful force. As he fearfully looked forward, a segment of an arm appeared in the middle of the air. With a triangular pattern extending on the arm, from the center of the hand, somehow the arm started to bend space. The suction force was more than imagined. As the arm was able to pull Gordom out of the spiral and more towards the arm.

Before Gordom could process what was happening, before he knew it he was absorbed into the arm. Gordom was robbed into another dimension with silence, because of the darkness it was extremely borderline impossible to see the exact happenings.

"Woah, what was that?" asked Scarlet.

"What was that mate?" questioned Erik.

"I sensed a huge amount of life energy just instantly disappearing without a strace. And the eerie thing is I cannot sense any of the same energy anymore." said Scarlet.

"Well, where was it mate?" asked Erik.

"It was extremely close to us, maybe 10 meters away from me," said Scarlet.

"Well, are you sure you didn't make a mistake, mate?" asked Erik.

"I'm extremely unsure as to how that much amount of energy can be stored in a small entity," said Scarlet.

As Scarlet was quite baffled by this occurrence, however, what they both don't know is that the disappearing presence was Gordom.

# CHAPTER 21

The slim and dark creature was getting closer and closer by time. And the closer it gets, the less conscious David is. However despite the danger, Hoseki was dead silent. Which was quite strange as David's life is more important to Hoseki than David himself.

Suddenly, David felt an immense amount of energy overtaking the control of his body. David had lost complete control over his endangered body. It had seemed like David was kicked out of his own body.

There were strange changes to David's body. There was a blue crystal horn on David's forehead. And throughout his body there were small crystals all around his body.

"Relax, you dirty scoundrel of a creature," said David.

David's voice was slightly different, as he can hear the voice of Hoseki combined with his own voice.

The creature went in for the last punch to finish off David. Suddenly, there was a glare in David's eye. Somehow David arrogantly dodged the hit and somehow was able to quickly glide to the left of the creature. The creature's hand was stuck to the wall as it was able to penetrate through metal infused graphene.

With seconds apart, David had another bright glare in his eye. David threw his fist toward the creature's head. The punch was so powerful that it was able to crush its head instantly on contact.

With glass like material shattering everywhere, somehow the shattered parts began to reform the creature again. With the parts flying back to its original form, David backed up as he watched the reformation.

Before the creature could complete its reform process, David suddenly formed a crystalized sword by a flash of time.

David slashed the sword right across the center of the creature. A trace of light appeared in David's eye.

The creature instantly shattered once it made contact with the sword. However, this time the shattered parts did not reform to its original form.

Instantly, David collapsed onto the ground. His body felt extremely heavy, at the state that he is right now, moving will not be possible.

"What was that?" David struggled.

"I can't explain everything right now. I have used way too much energy." responded Hoseki in a dull tone.

David seemingly got control over his body, however he could not move. It had seemed like every atom in his body had been worn out. It felt like every muscle in his body had been used to their max. As every part of David's body was aching and muscle tension went through the roof. Though David could not feel the extreme pain aching in his body. David felt something worse.

The toll that is taking in his brain is overwhelming. It felt like he was hallucinating the most. Everything felt unreal at the moment. David was seeing random patterns through his fading eyesight.

Without much energy left, David shutted his eyes and willinging fainted into needed rest.

Suddenly, in the corners of the room, something started moving slowly. Crumbling noise started appearing on the opposite side of the room. Shatter glass slowly moving toward one place.

With one last leap of energy, David slowly opened his eyes. Seeing the glass reform into the dark figure for the one last time. Then, David faded into unconsciousness.

# CHAPTER 22

Gordom felt extreme dizziness as he was basically sucked from a wormhole to another by pure force. A feeling of sickness exploded from inside out. It felt like his organs were being torn out and his brain was being smashed against a concrete wall. With extreme discomfort he found himself laying on the cold ground of some kind of room.

The only visible thing in the room was the floor. As it had felt like the ground was floating in nothingness void.

There was Gordom, carelessly thrown onto the ground. Powerlessly laying on the cold floor.

Gordom's body felt heavy. His mind defies gravity. It felt like his body was going through evolution in a matter of seconds. It had felt like all his bones were moving through Gordom's flesh and blood.

With extreme pain, Gordom was lifted into the air by a strange force. A certain amount of pressure could be felt on his calf. Though nothing visible was there to create the pressure.

Something caught his eyes, there was another black platform on the opposite side of one Gordom was standing on. However, there was a pool of green glowing on the black platform. Despite it being upside down, the liquid was not moving a single bit.

With Gordom elevating closer to the platform, he felt two extremely intense forces clashing into each other. Suddenly, Gordom was tossed into the pool of bright green liquid.

Instantly with direct contact with the liquid, Gordom could feel minor amounts of comfort and pleasure. The feeling of warming flustered into Gordom's body. He felt his body quickly regenerating energy.

It was a strange and eerie feeling, as it felt like his body was slowly coming back into its original form. His inner organs were seemingly being restored from the deformation. Moments passed with Gordom still powerlessly floating on the pool of liquid.

Gordom was able to regain some strength and consciousness. His arms were barely able to move again. With some consciousness regained, Gordom was bewildered by the situation he was in.

Even though he gained some of his energy, movement was still a problem. Gordom looked around to see himself in the middle of nowhere, laying in a pool of green liquid on a floating platform. As Gordom struggled to make out where he was, a figure appeared in the near distance.

Gordom couldn't make out the appearance of the figure. It had seemed like the figure had blended its body in with the surroundings. The figure seemingly glided towards Gordom.

As the figure got closer and closer, its appearance became more and more confusing. What it appeared to be was that the figure had no actual body. Gordom could only see a floating white mask, a white tall hat, a pair of white gloves and a white cape. As the other parts of its body were not visible.

Suddenly, the figure disappeared, in an instant it was gone. It had seemed like the being just faded away from existence. The trace of his being just disappeared.

A vein of coldness creeped from Gordom's back.

It slowly sank into Gordom's skin. As an eerie feeling deepens into Gordom's mind. Gordom's eye slipped and caught a glimpse behind him.

A white mask floating midair. Gordom could see the details of the mask, as it was a thalia mask.

Seconds later, the mask faded into darkness, leaving Gordom lost in a sea of confusion.

Gordom slowly got out of the pool of green liquids. The strangeness was that Gordom got out of the pool completely dry. Despite being soaked in the pool, every part of his body was unmoisturized.

Gordom made his way onto the surface and lay vulnerable on the ground. As the process of getting out of the pool took a huge toll on his body. This leaves him physically incapable on the cold floor. Incapable of doing basically anything, his physical state of being can be considered dead. However, Gordom's conscious state can be considered another living being, as the will power of its conscious being was more than 9000.

However, Gordom still could not comprehend what the thalia mask was and how it had just appeared out of nowhere.

From the back of his mind, a rush of feeling arose. As he felt an extreme rush of heat forming inside his body. As it had felt like every vein and muscle in his body was pumped.

With an immense amount of unknown energy flooding his body, Gordom felt like his body was going to melt. With much heat in his body, a strange feeling of coldness sunk into his body. Even though his body was blazing hot, a cold feeling deepened into his body.

Despite the strange reaction of his body, Gordom was able to easily stand up. Though he was able to stand up, there was not much in his surroundings. With Gordom on a floating black platform in the middle of nowhere.

The area gave Gordom an eerie and uncomfortable vibe. It felt like it had a heavy scent of sadness and loneliness, yet having just a small scent of happiness and excitement. However, the happiness felt alone. It felt like happiness was built on others. It felt like happiness was just a shallow cover that protects what is empty under it.

*"Hehehehe"* cried a sharp voice in the distance.

"Who was that?" projected Gordom.

Suddenly a white figure flashed in the background. Slowly figures of whiteness start flashing around Gordom. Quick vague flashes continuously circled Gordom.

"*HEHEHEHEHE*" boomed a voice.

Seemingly taunting Gordom, the figure got closer to Gordom. Suddenly, a blind force pushed Gordom onto the ground.

"*Get up weakling*"

Gordom attempted to get up, however another blind force plunged Gordom onto the hard floor. As Gordom looked up, it had seemed like the figures were laughing at him.

"*Oi, when are you gonna get up?*" said the voice as Gordom is seemingly punched by an unknown force.

Gordom not responding, lunged himself toward one of the flashing figures. However, Gordom was met with the cold hard floor again. Gordom seemingly flew right through the figure.

"*HA! The weakling couldn't even get up, yet he tried to touch ME. What an idiot.*" said the voice.

"Who are you?" shouted Gordom angrily

"Who am I, may you ask. The fact that you don't know angers me deeply. I did not become this powerful to be disrespected by a meritless mortal. You shall have to learn who I am."

A colorless fog emerged around Gordom, a chilling breeze encompassed the atmosphere. Suddenly, sound screeched into Gordom's ears. It was a strange mixture of sounds, what happens to sound like a woman weeping mixed with the cries of a child. With glimpses of holograms of faceless figures, Gordom was trapped with confusion.

As the fog became dense and denser, Gordom attempted to dissemble the fog. However, he was not able to move. He caught his body trembling without his acknowledgment. It had seemed like Gordom had lost complete control over his body. His body shaking violently, Gordom felt his knees weak. His joints loose, and his mind blank.

Suddenly, Gordom felt something cold on his arm. Something slowly crawling up his arm. Perhaps a liquid, as the cold yet smooth feeling crawls up Gordom's arm. It was extremely difficult to move, Gordom used extreme force to tilt his head just a little. With much resistance, Gordom was able to see a figure.

However, the figure was different. It gave off a rotten smell. A black liquid slowly crawled its way up Gordom's arm. It gave off a weird feeling, the higher the liquid got. The parts it covered, Gordom could no longer feel. It felt like his arm fell clean off. All Gordom could do was stand there in fear. Once the liquid got up to his shoulders, it felt like his arm disappeared into the thin air. The weight of the arm was gone, the temperature became room temperature. The liquid began to reveal Gordom's hand. However, his hand was not there. His hand disappeared.

Gordom could not believe it, there was no pain at all. It was as if it just evaporated into thin air.

Gordom screamed in fear, hoping that none of this was reality. However, it had seemed like it was. It had seemed like Gordom had lost an arm.

Suddenly, he felt pain in his stomach. It felt like something piercing through his stomach.

"WAKE UP CHILD" screamed someone.

Suddenly, Gordom found himself on the cold floor. He looked down, he found his arm was still there. With a sigh of relief, he stayed on the ground for a few seconds.

"Weakling, you don't even compare to me." said someone

As Gordom looked up, it was an invisible figure with a white suit, cape, tall hat, and gloves. The figure lifted his fingers, and suddenly Gordom felt someone grab his neck. Gordom was lifted up into the air. He tried to release the force that was grabbing him, however there was nothing there.

"You see how weak you are compared to me?" questioned the figure.

"Let me go " struggled Gordom.

The figure pointed his finger to the right, Gordom was thrown into the distant right.

"Realize how weak and pitiful you are, and speak to me with respect!" yelled the figure.

The figure lifted his fingers again. This time upwards. Gordom flew up into the air instantly. Leaving the ground almost two hundred feet in the air in the matter of 2 seconds.

After a few seconds, the figure pointed his fingers downward. Gordom was launched right back onto the ground. Gordom screamed in extreme pain.

However, Gordom quickly got up and lunged at the figure. Attempting to attack him, but the figure reacted too quickly. The figure with another wave of a figure sent Gordom flying in another direction.

"Hmm, impressive. That fall would have killed you." said the figure.

"You.. are madly... underestimating me" stuttered Gordom.

"Hmm, then I shall test you to your limits." said the figure.

The figure grasped his hand and formed it into a ball.

For once, Gordom was actually scared of what was to come. As he does not know his power's limits and in any second he could fall from grace.

"Are you ready, pity mortal?" questioned the figure.

Suddenly, the figure released his hand. Nothing happened at first, however, suddenly, his body began heating up extremely fast. His arm and legs began to feel extremely stretched. A blind force continues to stretch out Gordom's body. Every inch of his body felt tense, even the inside of his body. At any point, Gordom felt his body would explode.

"Let me go " struggled Gordom.

The figure pointed his finger to the right, Gordom was thrown into the distant right.

"Realize how weak and pitiful you are, and speak to me with respect!" yelled the figure.

The figure lifted his fingers again. This time upwards. Gordom flew up into the air instantly. Leaving the ground almost two hundred feet in the air in the matter of 2 seconds.

After a few seconds, the figure pointed his fingers downward. Gordom was launched right back onto the ground. Gordom screamed in extreme pain.

However, Gordom quickly got up and lunged at the figure. Attempting to attack him, but the figure reacted too quickly. The figure with another wave of a figure sent Gordom flying in another direction. Suddenly, a bright flash blinded Gordom momentarily.

As Gordom lost sight, loud sounds boomed beyond infinity. Sounds of lightning and explosions blared across the sky. Seconds later, Gordom was able to retrieve his eyesight back. What was there put fear in his stomach.

# CHAPTER 23

The shattered glass began to reform once again. The shattered glass stacked second by second. The glass slowly rumbled towards David's unconscious body. The closer the glass got, the more complete the monster became.

David could do nothing, his unconscious inner being laid there with impotentness.

The creature's incomplete body slowly stumbled across the quiet room. The monster became closer and more complete second by second.

However, David could do nothing but lay there powerlessly waiting for his end.